## "I've wanted to see you how grateful I am..."

"Jasmine—"

Her heart leaped, but she was afraid, too. "But if you tell me you think I'm emotionally unstable because of the crash and don't know my own mind, then I'll get out of the truck right now and we won't be seeing each other again."

He leaned across and caught her softly rounded chin in his hand so she was forced to look him in the eyes. They'd darkened with emotion.

"When I was witness to the magnificent way you handled yourself at the crash site, I knew you were the most emotionally stable woman I would ever meet in my life!"

"Thank you for saying that." She wanted him to kiss her. Oh, how she wanted him to take her in his arms.

She was no longer the same woman who'd answered the front door.

The earth had turned on its axis because Wymon Clayton had happened to her...and nothing would ever be the same again.

Dear Reader,

Montana, the land of mountains, is still a wilderness where you can get out to see wildlife in their natural setting. I've spent years vacationing throughout the western part of the state from the Sapphire Mountains to West Yellowstone. Whether horseback riding or hiking, there's no sight more thrilling than coming across a trophy elk or a bull moose drinking at an ancient water hole early in the morning. There's nothing more incredible than coming across a mother grizzly bear with her cub ambling through the pines toward evening. The majesty of all God's creations comes alive at moments like these. In this novel, *Made for the Rancher*, I wanted to celebrate the wonder of two people who miraculously meet after an accident and fall madly in love in this incredible setting. Everyone should be so lucky to visit this part of the country at least once in their lives.

Enjoy!

Rebecca Winters

# MADE FOR THE RANCHER

**REBECCA WINTERS**

———

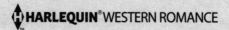

HARLEQUIN® WESTERN ROMANCE

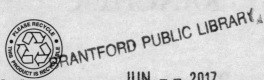

ISBN-13: 978-0-373-75758-9

Made for the Rancher

Copyright © 2017 by Rebecca Winters

This edition published by arrangement with Harlequin Books S.A.

For questions and comments about the quality of this book, please contact us at CustomerService@Harlequin.com.

HARLEQUIN®
www.Harlequin.com

Printed in U.S.A.

**Rebecca Winters**, whose family of four children has now swelled to include five beautiful grandchildren, lives in Salt Lake City, Utah, in the land of the Rocky Mountains. Living near canyons and high alpine meadows full of wildflowers, she never runs out of places to explore. They, plus her favorite vacation spots in Europe, often end up as backgrounds for her romance novels, because writing is her passion, along with her family and church.

Rebecca loves to hear from readers. If you wish to email her, please visit her website, cleanromances.com.

## Books by Rebecca Winters

### Harlequin Western Romance

#### *Sapphire Mountain Cowboys*

*A Valentine for the Cowboy*

#### *Lone Star Lawmen*

*The Texas Ranger's Bride*
*The Texas Ranger's Nanny*
*The Texas Ranger's Family*
*Her Texas Ranger Hero*

#### *Hitting Rocks Cowboys*

*In a Cowboy's Arms*
*A Cowboy's Heart*
*The New Cowboy*
*A Montana Cowboy*

Visit the Author Profile page
at Harlequin.com for more titles.

Dedicated to the memory of the great John Muir,
also known as John of the Mountains.
He was a Scottish-American naturalist,
author, environmental philosopher and
early advocate of the preservation of the
wilderness in the United States.

# *Chapter One*

"Mr. Clayton? I'm Ross Lee from KUSM-TV. Would you mind answering a few questions?"

Surprised to hear his name called out, Wymon glanced to his left. He'd just come from a committee meeting and had walked out onto the steps of the Montana State capitol building in Helena with his close friend Jim Whitefeather, only to have a microphone shoved in his face.

"Good news travels fast," Jim muttered. The two of them were disappointed that a final decision wouldn't be reached for another month when they would meet with the governor again. The eager-beaver reporter already suspected the worst outcome would happen in thirty days. No doubt he considered this delay good news.

Wymon and the members of the committee had been in the public eye for the last six months raising awareness of a controversial issue close to his heart. They'd welcomed the publicity to get their message across and had held debates across the state, some of which had been in the news.

On this day, however, he would have liked to ignore the negative attention. He and Jim needed to be diplomatic because their fight wasn't over. They had another month to convince the public that this issue was worth fighting for.

"Naturally I'd hoped for a positive decision today," Wymon told the reporter. "But I'm feeling confident that next month we *will* be successful."

He felt the reporter bristle. "With you being the head of the Sapphire Ranch, it's well known that you're one of the biggest proponents for the reintroduction of the grizzly bear to the Sapphire and Bitterroot wilderness in western Montana."

"That's right. My colleague here, Mr. James Whitefeather of the Nez Perce tribe, is another big proponent. We're part of a much larger group dedicated to fulfilling our initial mission statement."

"If you would, highlight it again for our television audience."

Taking the opportunity to speak on one of his favorite subjects, Wymon said, "Our vision is that one day the grizzly will once again have a population in northwest Montana. We want to see them interact with the greater Yellowstone area population to the south as they did hundreds of years ago when thousands of them lived here before being killed off."

"But, Mr. Clayton—as I understand it, today's lack of a decision means most voters in Montana believe the issue is on a downward spiral."

"All great ideas face setbacks," Wymon countered. "We're continually working to get the necessary votes. In a month's time we hope to win by a landslide."

The reporter squinted at him. "You think that's possible?"

"Anything's possible, and the decisions made by our committee will serve to guide the federal and state agencies involved in grizzly bear management. It's our belief that a new grizzly population will contribute to the balance and harmony of nature. It will also contribute significantly to long-term conservation and recovery of the species."

"What do you have to say in response to State Representative Farnsworth's attacks on your coalition? He claims that the majority of people are against reintroducing the *Ursus horribilis* to the area. This hot issue has had tempers flaring on both sides of the state border."

"A slender majority are currently against it." Wymon's jaw hardened in reaction. "I'd say the man who gave the species its scientific name had never encountered a grizzly outside of the Lewis and Clark reports. A damn shame considering it was rightly recognized as *Ursus arctos*, but the 'horrible' stuck, and the grizzly was forever mislabeled in the cruelest of ways."

"You question history?"

"Not history, just one man's uninformed opinion. I wonder how many people in your viewing audience realize that in the entire 142-year history of Yellowstone National Park, there have only been eight reported human deaths by bears, and not all of them have been proven to be by grizzlies. That's one in every seventeen years. The chances of being killed in a car accident or in a plane accident are so much greater—there's no contest.

"But to answer your question, I'll give you a quote from John Muir, the Scottish naturalist, who was an early advocate for preserving America's wilderness. He spent three nights in the forest with Teddy Roosevelt who had the foresight to establish our national parks. You know the story about how the teddy bear was named after him?"

"I can't say I do."

That didn't surprise Wymon. "His hunting party treed a small black bear and waited for Teddy to take the shot, but he decided that killing the young trapped bear wasn't sporting.

"To paraphrase a quote of Muir's on the grizzly, he said, 'He's neither an enemy nor a means to our spiritual development, neither something to conquer nor something to experience. He's simply an equal.'"

"An equal?"

"Yes. Muir said, 'Nature's object in making animals and plants might possibly be first of all the happiness of *each* one of them.'" Wymon emphasized the specific word.

The reporter frowned. "You mean they were created for their own happiness? Even the grizzly?"

"That's right." Jim took over to finish the quote. "'And *not* the creation of all plants and animals for the happiness of *one* who wants things his own way.' *That* is man's arrogance. A better title for him should be *Homo sapien horribilis*."

At the reporter's stunned expression, Wymon almost laughed out loud. He'd bought horses from his good friend Jim for several years. The man had a great sense of humor, which was very much in evidence at the moment.

Jim kept talking. "Consider that Montana has fifteen mountain ranges above six thousand feet in seventeen counties that include, among others, the Bitterroot, Garnet, Big Belt and Sapphire. All were the natural habitat for the now-dead grizzlies who have every right to be here today."

Wymon muttered "Amen" under his breath. "Now you'll have to excuse us. We've got to get to the airport." He and Jim left the confused-looking reporter to grill the others coming out of the meeting and hurried down the steps in the June heat to a waiting limo.

During the short ride they talked business. Next week they would meet again and figure out a ground game to reach every voter in Montana and Idaho. Wymon also planned to go up in the mountains with a couple of the wildlife experts and rangers to discuss a new conflict management program to put in place.

One of their biggest priorities was to discuss the uncertainty of the survival outlook for translocated grizzlies. There was also the problem of capturing enough sub-adult females to meet the shortened time frame when they were in heat.

Once they reached the airport, Jim got on a plane to fly back to his family in Missoula. Wymon took a flight to Stevensville, a small town in Ravalli County in the western part of Montana. From there he'd drive his truck to the ranch five miles away.

It was a good thing Wymon's brother Eli had married recently and was running the ranch on a full-time basis. It allowed Wymon to focus on finding the funding necessary to revitalize the program he and his friends had instituted the year before.

No doubt it would take a hundred years at least to see his vision realized. Wymon would be dead before then, but he and Jim were in lockstep to help secure a recovered population of grizzly bears that would one day include a core of five hundred or more in the northern Continental Divide area.

They both envisioned grizzly bear management similar to the management of other resident species that maintained effective biological connections all the way from Canada in the north to the Bitterroot Sapphire area.

He'd been excited about the idea of bringing grizzlies back since his youth when he'd spent time in the mountains with his father and they'd talked about their demise. His dad had lamented their loss, and his concerns had served to ignite a fire in Wymon who vowed that when he got old enough, he'd try to make a difference.

If time had permitted before leaving the steps of the capitol, Wymon would have liked to relate another of Muir's many journal entries that had always stood out in his mind.

*The night before I left Yellowstone, I found myself in a small crowd squinting at a distant hillside.*

*A grizzly was eating an elk carcass, while a wolf lay in wait just a few meters away. When the bear was sated, she simply rambled off, leaving the carcass behind. The coast now clear, the wolf jaunted over to dig in.*

*The crowd there urged the bear to react: "Fight!" at least two people cried, craving some carnal satisfaction in sharp teeth and bloody jaws. The bear, thank goodness, paid us no mind, leaving the wolf free to keep tugging at the meat.*

*According to a park ranger, the wolf would bring some back to feed his pups. And the grizzly, with the wolf gone, would return. And so it would continue, two apex predators accepting the other's presence, engaged in an ongoing dance of wary respect.*

That was the kind of respect Wymon hoped those dissenters of the plan—like Representative Farnsworth's constituency—would develop in time. What it would take was more information at their disposal *and* the money to pay helpers for their ground game of dissemination of pamphlets and video clips produced for the public.

As he drove under the antler arch of the Clayton cattle ranch entrance, he looked up at the majestic Sapphire Mountains behind it, mountains filled with sapphires created at the dawn of time, sapphires his family had mined for years.

His eyes burned with hot tears. Wymon missed his father like hell. Maybe it was better he wasn't alive to hear that today's bill had been postponed. But Wymon had no intention of giving up.

AFTER GETTING OFF the phone with Rob, Jasmine Telford sank down on the side of her bed, wishing she hadn't told him she'd go with him. But he said he'd be there at 8:30 a.m., so she couldn't back out now.

Her gaze strayed to the small suitcase she'd just packed. She'd never gone away with him overnight, but he'd been hinting that this was something important for his career. He'd sounded so serious that she'd agreed to take the day off from her job at the university. But she'd told him they would have to have separate bedrooms. She'd never been to bed with a man and didn't have those feelings for him.

Rob Farnsworth, an energy engineer from Helena, was running for a second term as a state representative. She'd met him three months ago in her father's office, and he'd instantly won over her parents with his charm and intelligence. As for her, she wasn't so sure, but from that time on he'd pursued her with a vengeance. At first she was flattered, but after a while little things about him started to bother her. He'd been indulged by his wealthy family—and she discovered that his ambition, like theirs, went beyond Montana politics, which made her nervous.

She'd come from a ranching family. Though her dad had been involved in local politics, he planned to get back to the family feed business once he was out of office. Her hardworking father was serving his last term as a state public service commissioner.

Jasmine's mother was always right at his side supporting him and often stayed with him in Helena when he had business there, only coming home to

Philipsburg on the odd weekend. That left Jasmine, who still lived at home, on her own.

Heaving a sigh, she phoned her mother and got her voice mail. Jasmine left a message saying that she was going out of town with Rob and would be back the next day, but that she'd stay in touch.

Before Rob arrived, she went in the bathroom to refresh her coral lipstick and run a brush through her wavy dark blond hair that was naturally streaked by the sun. She kept it medium-short so it didn't need a lot of work.

He'd said to dress casually, so she'd put on designer jeans and a short-sleeved khaki blouse. After slipping on her leather sandals, she put on some lemon-scented lotion and decided she was ready.

Within seconds she heard him honk and left the house with her suitcase. Rob got out to hug her and take her bag. "I hope you're up for an airplane ride."

*No-o.* Her head lifted. "You're kidding."

"Why would I do that? I've been asking you to fly with me for a long time, and you've always turned me down. But I'm not going to let you get away with it today. By the way, you look beautiful." He planted a firm kiss on her mouth, but his plans had caught her off guard.

"Hey—" His brown eyes swept over her. "What's wrong? I thought you told me you're not afraid of flying."

"I'm not."

"So, it's just me you don't trust. Honey, I logged two thousand flying hours in the military."

"Trust has nothing to do with it. I've said no because you fly for your job. I haven't wanted to interfere with that."

He frowned. "Interfere? I want you with me whenever possible. Remember that huge rally scheduled in Helena in three weeks? You promised you'd come with me and my parents."

"I know." She *had* promised him. But since then she'd become less sure about their relationship. "I'll fly with you this one time, Rob, but that's it." While they were on this trip, she'd tell him she would rather not be at his political rally.

Rob stowed her case in the rental car, and they took off for Riddick Field Airport in Philipsburg where he'd flown in from Helena. She saw a plane she didn't recognize sitting out on the runway.

"That's yours?"

"It's a Cessna 177B single-engine plane."

"You got a new one?"

"That's my surprise!" He grinned at her, reminding her of a kid on Christmas. "Nothing but the best when you buy a Cessna Cardinal. She's a four-seater and a real honey of a serious cross-country machine. She's got 180 horse power. You're going to love it."

Before long they reached the parking area. He walked her to the shiny blue-and-white plane and introduced her to his mechanic. They shook hands. "You're going up on a beautiful day, Ms. Telford."

"It is gorgeous out."

Rob helped her onboard. "As you can see, there's a

lot of room in a Cardinal. Take out the backseat and you can fit camping gear for three weeks. It's really amazing. We can get two folding bikes, kid seats and a cooler behind the backseat for a full-family day trip, or fit a family of four in here with all the ski gear, no problem."

Whoa. His mind was taking their relationship to a whole new level. When he'd said this outing was important for his career, she hadn't realized *she* was a part of it. Whatever he was leading up to, she wasn't ready for anything that serious. Jasmine still didn't know him well enough yet, not after three months. And what she did know raised certain concerns in her mind.

Pretty soon they were settled and both put on their headgear. He turned to her with a smile. "We're flying to Seattle and won't be back until Sunday."

"The whole weekend?"

"I have a little business to do there. How does that sound?"

"You've surprised me. I haven't been there in years," she said to cover what she'd really wanted to say, that she'd rather not go.

"Good. I have it all planned out."

Rob was a planner with enough drive for three people. That was why he'd been so successful in business and politics. Besides his good looks, he had many admirable qualities, but that drive he'd inherited from his parents made her nervous.

Did he ever slow down? Have a quiet moment? Maybe spending the weekend with him would help her figure out if he could just be still and enjoy life. So far she suspected he was a workaholic. Jasmine wondered if she could live with a person like that, never mind that he might take exception to her more laid-back personality.

After starting the engine, he was cleared for take-off. Soon the land receded, and they headed into a picture-perfect blue sky. Philipsburg lay below between two mountain ranges filled with mining ghost towns and lakes that made the scenery a never-ending tapestry of beauty.

"We're flying over a portion of the Sapphires on our way," he explained after they'd reached cruising altitude. "Did I tell you we're finally showing some real progress on getting rid of the pollution from the old mines?"

"Yes." She chuckled. He couldn't help talking about his ideas for cleaning up the rivers to help the fish population thrive.

"I'm happy about the decline in the wolf population, too. Wolves are on a downward trend in the area. It means the tools we're using to manage them are effective. The impact we're making there is positive, and there's more good news. The bill to reintroduce grizzlies into the area was postponed for a month due to pressure from our side. That particular ranching coalition is a tough group, but we've prevailed so far."

"I know you were strongly against it." Jasmine looked down at the green canopy below. When she was young and on a hike with her parents, she remembered seeing a grizzly with her two cubs up in the Coffin Lakes area. Her father had whispered, "Isn't she a magnificent animal?" Her mother had replied, "And she's a good mother, too."

"They have no place in today's world." Rob kept talking while she was still thinking about that campout with her folks. "There's enough trauma without inviting more. Fortunately, enough of my constituents agree with me."

She felt like changing the subject. "When was the last time you took a real vacation?"

"It's been a while, but there never seems to be enough time."

"That's because you thrive on work."

"Don't you?"

"Not in the same way." It wasn't a career that consumed her day and night.

"Why do I get the feeling you resent me for it, and that's why you haven't flown with me until now."

"That's not true at all," she said. "Please, don't think that. To love your work makes you who you are. I'm so impressed by your energy and excitement."

"Impressed enough to want to be my wife?"

There it was! The question she'd been dreading. She hadn't expected it right this second and clasped her hands in her lap.

"Rob—"

After a silence he said, "That wasn't the one-word answer I wanted to hear. I knew you were the one for me when we first met. Surely you've realized I'm in love with you, Jasmine."

She wished she could say the same, but she

couldn't. "I care for you a lot, Rob. Otherwise I wouldn't be with you now, but—"

"But your feelings aren't strong enough to say you'll marry me," he broke in on her.

"I need more time to commit to a decision that will change my whole life."

"How much more? I'd hoped we'd return from our trip with the engagement ring I bought for you on your finger. I want it there when we attend the rally in three weeks. It's a good thing I know your feelings now instead of at dinner when I'd planned to propose to you."

Her heart sank. "I'm so sorry, Rob. The last thing I want to do is hurt you. I've always been slower to make any important decision. It's my nature. You know I think you're wonderful, or I wouldn't have come with you."

She felt horrible and wished she *hadn't* agreed to come with him. Now she'd ruined the weekend. In the silence she suddenly heard a thump and then there was a burst of feathers in the cockpit. A bird had crashed through the windshield. The propeller fluttered before the engine died.

Jasmine cried out Rob's name, but his focus was on the controls, pushing in knobs, pulling out others. He turned to her. "We've hit a hawk, and now we're going to have to put her down in the mountains."

"We're going to crash, aren't we?"

"Afraid so, but we have about ninety seconds before we reach the treetops. After impact, we have to get out as quickly as we can. If I'm unconscious, remember to pull these latches to get out of your seat belt and get me out of mine. You need to get away from the plane as fast as possible. Now I want you to cover your head with your arms."

She turned straight forward in a state of shock while she heard him call, "Mayday, Mayday, Mayday." Jasmine couldn't believe this was happening to them.

"Look—right over there. A logging road that might open into a small meadow. I'm going to head for that. Let's pray she glides to the opening, and we don't hit the trees."

While Jasmine was praying with all her might, she heard him repeat, "Come on, come on. I don't know if we're going to make it, but we're going to try."

The next thing she was aware of was the crush of branches, and she realized the tail was raking through the trees. All of a sudden she was thrown forward in her seat, and the plane hit the ground. In that horrific moment it slid up a slope to a stop.

Amazed she was still alive, she turned to Jim. His head lay against the side window. She cried his name, but he didn't respond. He'd been knocked out, but she didn't see any blood except some cuts on his hands and arms. It took her a minute to think.

*If I'm unconscious, remember to pull the latches to get out of your seat belt.*

She followed his instructions and reached for the latch to extricate herself. Then she pulled his latch. He still wasn't moving. She felt for a pulse. He was still alive, thank God.

She had to get them out of there, but when she tried to open her door, it wouldn't budge. She tried again before realizing it had been dented on impact and would need force in order to pry it open.

The only thing to do was climb out the shattered windshield and jump down so she could pull him out of the plane on his side. First she had to push out the broken glass so she wouldn't cut herself exiting the cockpit.

With her adrenaline gushing, she cleared it enough to get through, then climbed up on the seat. After gripping part of the dented frame, she swung herself through and took a leap. The ground came up hard, almost knocking the wind out of her. Nausea swept through her. When she could find the strength to stand, she hurried around to the pilot's side of the plane.

She reached for the door handle and opened it. Jim was six feet and a dead weight in her arms. She tried to work him out of his seat belt. If he had internal injuries or a broken neck or bones, she had no way of knowing. All that mattered was to get them as far away from the plane as possible before something exploded.

## Chapter Two

Wymon had been driving along one of the logging roads in the Sapphires for about ten minutes when he saw a single engine plane plunge into the trees directly ahead of him.

His heart almost failed him. He reached for his phone and called 911. After identifying himself, he gave the coordinates of the crash. "I'm headed to the site. Send an ambulance and a Bronco with a tank of water ASAP."

Another minute and he reached a clearing where he saw a wrecked Cessna and a blonde woman working to pull the pilot from the cockpit. No fire had broken out yet—there was just a trail of ripped-up ground made by the plane when it came down. Amazed that part of it was still intact, he knew a crack pilot had been at the controls.

He jumped out of his truck and ran to help. "I'll take over, but first I need to get you to safety. My name is Wymon Clayton." He picked up the woman and carried her to the edge of the clearing.

"Thank you. He still has a pulse," she yelled after him as he ran toward the plane.

Wymon pulled the pilot free of his harness and dragged him as fast as he could toward the woman. The poor guy was covered in cuts from the broken windshield. Oddly enough, he looked familiar to Wymon. Once he'd reached her, he began CPR.

"Come on, Rob. Wake up," she cried.

Rob. This was Robert Farnsworth, a state representative who'd been vocal about the drainage cleanup from the mines. Wymon could understand that, but more recently he'd been against the grizzly reintroduction issue which went against what Wymon was fighting for.

He continued giving him CPR. In another minute the pilot came to.

"Oh thank God, you're awake!" the woman said and smoothed the hair off his forehead.

"Jasmine?" he said faintly.

"Don't move, Mr. Farnsworth. An ambulance is on its way." He looked into the woman's beautiful spring-green eyes. She'd survived an ordeal that should have knocked her out too, or worse. Cuts covered part of her arms, as well. "Make him lie still while I run for a blanket."

Wymon raced to the truck. He pulled two blankets from the truck bed where he always kept his camping gear for emergencies and reached for a can of soda from the rear seat. When he returned, he put one blanket over the pilot to keep him warm, and then told the woman to sit down. He was surprised she hadn't gone into shock already. Once she'd done as he asked, he wrapped the other blanket around her. In the process, his face brushed against her sweet-smelling hair.

"Drink this. You need the sugar."

"Thank you," she said in a quiet voice. "If you hadn't come when you did…"

"Don't think about that."

He moved over to the pilot and hunkered down next to him. "The paramedics will be here any moment. Are you feeling severe pain anywhere besides your head?"

"No. A hawk… It flew into the propeller and shattered the windshield."

"You deserve a medal for getting both of you out of this crash alive. There aren't that many open pockets in this area."

"Rob's an incredible pilot," his companion acknowledged. "He told me exactly what to do." She took a few more sips of the drink.

He glanced at her, noting that she wasn't wearing a ring. "You were brave to try to pull him away from the plane." As he spoke, several ambulances from Stevensville and the Bronco he'd called for drove into view.

The driver recognized Wymon and called out to him. Quick as lightning, two of the men with him started draining fuel from the wings of the plane in the hope of preventing a fire. Another one got busy removing the battery.

To Wymon's relief, the paramedics came running

over to take care of the crash victims. "I'm all right," the woman said. "It's Rob who needs help."

"He's getting it," Wymon told her. "But you need to be checked out, too. Let the paramedics do their job."

They worked with both of them while getting names and addresses. Wymon discovered the woman's name was Jasmine Telford. She lived in Philipsburg. The name Telford rang another bell. He knew why when one of the paramedics murmured to his partner that she was related to Commissioner Telford and did legal work for a friend of his.

Digesting that information, Wymon hurried over to the plane to take pictures inside and out with his cell phone. Soon the patients were placed on stretchers and ready to be transported to the hospital. He recovered his blankets and walked beside Jasmine to the ambulance. "I'll follow you to the hospital and make sure you and Mr. Farnsworth get your luggage back."

"Thank you again for everything you've done."

"I'm only glad I happened to be driving up here today." He'd been on his way to meeting with some rangers, but that was obviously not happening anymore.

The paramedics lifted Jasmine inside the ambulance and shut the door. Wymon walked over to the other ambulance. "I'll see you at the hospital, Mr. Farnsworth. Anything I can do, just let me know," he said, not expecting a reply.

Wymon got into his truck and followed the ambulances down the logging road that led back to Stevensville.

A sigh escaped him, and he thought that you never knew what was going to happen when you got up in the morning. He checked his watch. Eleven thirty and he was suddenly headed for the hospital. When he got there, he'd call the ranger station and explain why he'd never made it.

Once in town, he pulled in to the hospital's public parking area and entered the emergency entrance behind the paramedics. While both patients were transferred to cubicles and attended to, Wymon held on to their luggage.

Two police officers who knew him came inside to ask him questions since he'd been the one to call 911. After they'd talked to the patients, they left, leaving Wymon to wait until the doctor had seen to both Rob and Jasmine. It was Dr. Turner, the husband of a close friend of his brother Eli's wife. They'd met at Eli and Brianna's wedding in March.

"Wymon? Good to see you. I understand you were the knight in shining armor. Ms. Telford's words, not mine."

He scoffed. "How is she doing?"

"Surprisingly well for surviving a plane crash. We're cleaning up her cuts and will watch her for a while, but I expect she can be released in a few hours, barring any complications."

Relieved to hear that, he asked about Mr. Farnsworth.

"Representative Farnsworth suffered a blow to

the forehead, but no broken bones or internal damage. So far, so good. We'll do a CAT scan and an MRI, then put him in a private room. He'll have to stay overnight, maybe several nights to recover from his concussion.

"After what I found out in talking with her, they dodged several bullets today. She said he'd been a pilot in the military, and *you* pulled him out of the plane to give him CPR. Because you took care of them at the crash site, they're both in amazing shape considering what happened."

"I didn't do much. Can I go in to see her? I've got their luggage. She'll probably want a change of clothes."

"Of course. We'll talk later."

Wymon picked up the suitcases and walked down to Jasmine's cubicle. "Ms. Telford?"

"Yes? Come in."

He removed his sunglasses and pulled the curtain aside. His wandering eyes took in the sight of her lying in the bed with her blonde head raised. She was a natural beauty with her classic features. Even in a hospital gown, or because of it, her shapely figure was evident beneath the sheet. Her cuts had been tended to. She looked to be in her midtwenties, but age could be deceiving.

"You don't mind? I've brought in your cases."

"You're our savior, Mr. Clayton," she said with a warm smile. "The doctor said he knew you and wasn't at all surprised that the head of the Sapphire Ranch was the one to help us."

"His wife and my new sister-in-law are close friends." He set the cases by the wall before snagging a chair with his boot. "I understand Mr. Farnsworth will have to stay in the hospital for a few days, but you'll be released soon. How can I help?"

"You've already saved our lives."

"That's nonsense."

"No." She shook her head. "If you hadn't called 911 and come when you did, I wouldn't have been able to pull Rob out of the cockpit by myself. The plane could have burst into flames. I don't even want to think about what could have happened."

Neither did he. "Tell me something. How did you get out of the plane? I took pictures, and your side was so dented the guys had to use a crowbar to pry it open."

"I was desperate to get Rob out of the plane and crawled out the broken windshield."

"You're lucky you didn't cut yourself more or break your leg jumping down. Because of your bravery, both of you will live to see another day."

His admiration for her was as intense as his unwitting attraction. He hadn't been this strongly drawn to a woman in years.

JASMINE COULDN'T HELP staring at the tall, fit, gorgeous cowboy dressed in a Western shirt sitting next to her. She'd seen him in the news recently, fighting to reintroduce grizzly bears to the area. Rob had been fighting against them, but this man had always been with a group of ranchers, and she'd never seen him up close before.

Her breath caught when he took off his cowboy hat, revealing wavy black hair. Below black eyebrows, his light gray eyes were fringed with thick black lashes. With his chiseled jaw, the kind that didn't seem real, he had to be the most attractive man she'd ever seen in her life!

"Your hotshot pilot knew what to do to bring you home safely, Ms. Telford. He's to be commended."

She blinked. For a minute she was so blown away by him, she lost the thread of their conversation.

*Rob wasn't her hotshot pilot.* But he was always in the news, and at this point she realized both men had come up against each other on more than one occasion. She could see why this man considered Rob a hotshot type. He flew his own plane and was an outspoken legislator on his way to the top.

After having turned down Rob's marriage proposal, she wasn't sure how things were going to be between them once he'd recovered.

"He definitely saved our lives by knowing where to put us down. I need to let his parents know what has happened."

"I'm positive the police have already informed his family. The news will go out over the airwaves soon enough."

One of the female technicians came in with some juice and checked Jasmine's vital signs. "Are you hungry?"

"Not yet, but this tastes good."

"Let me know if you need anything."

"Do you know how Mr. Farnsworth is doing?"

"They're still running tests on him. I'll tell the doctor to give you an update when he can."

"Thank you."

She noticed the other woman check out Wymon Clayton before she walked out. In truth, Jasmine had been doing the same thing and had observed that he didn't wear any rings. She found herself wanting to know more about him.

"How did you happen to be in the mountains this morning?"

"I was on my way to meet up with some rangers on business, which reminds me I need to contact them and let them know why I didn't make it. If you'll excuse me, I'll be right back."

She wanted to tell him she didn't expect him to come back. He'd done more than enough for them, but he'd slipped behind the curtain before she could stop him. Once he'd gone, the doctor came back in and checked on her again.

"You're free to get up, use the bathroom, get dressed. Then you can go see Mr. Farnsworth if you like. If you're still feeling well in another hour, I'll release you."

"That's good. I'm anxious to move around now."

When she came out of the bathroom a few minutes later, Wymon Clayton was waiting for her. It shouldn't have excited her, but it did. His glance took in the jeans and knit top she'd pulled from her suitcase to wear, sending a slow burn through her body.

He stood there with his hat on. "The doctor told me you're free to walk around. Why don't you and I go to the cafeteria for a late lunch while we wait for Mr. Farnsworth to come back from his CAT scan?"

It was an innocent invitation offered by the man who'd come along in time to help save their lives, but she felt guilty when she said, "That sounds good. I think I'm getting hungry at last."

All she took with her was her phone from the bedside table before leaving the ER with him. He seemed to know exactly where to go. She noticed that women young and old eyed him up as they made their way to the cafeteria at the other end of the building. Jasmine was five foot seven, but she felt small compared to Wymon. He had to be over six feet and was taller than Rob.

She felt wrong comparing him with Rob, but she supposed it was natural that she'd notice the differences between the two men.

Jasmine and Wymon each took a tray and went through the line picking out what they felt like eating. He paid for their food and led them to a table in the corner.

"I'll pay you back when we get back to the room," she said.

He helped her settle into her chair before sitting down opposite her. "I'm the one who asked you to eat with me."

So he had. He had a quiet air of authority when he spoke, which had come across on TV. Again she got the sensation that she was doing something wrong.

The first time it had happened, she didn't know why, but this time she knew exactly what was disturbing her.

She felt an attraction to this man that was so much stronger than anything she'd ever felt before. Pure chemistry, hormones, whatever it was, it was powerful.

*Keep it casual, Jasmine. Just be grateful for his help, that's all. Remember the man you've been dating is getting a CAT scan right now—the man who wants to marry you and is still waiting for the right answer you can't give him.*

"Where were you headed when the hawk flew into you?"

She'd just swallowed another bite of her grilled ham-and-cheese sandwich. "Seattle."

"That's tough luck. At least insurance will pay for a new plane because it was an accident. Unfortunately, I'm sure that's small comfort for him at the moment."

"You're right. He just bought this plane."

"I'm sorry."

"Me, too." Sorry she'd hurt Rob so terribly right before the accident happened. He had to be suffering for a myriad of reasons. Her greatest hope was that nothing truly serious had happened to him except the concussion. You could recover fully from a concussion.

"More coffee?"

"Yes, please."

Wymon poured her some from the carafe. "I know he's an influential representative."

"A very dedicated one as I'm sure you've found out, being on the other side of the grizzly bear issue. How about you? Did you always want to be a rancher?"

He finished the rest of his coffee. "It's my life."

She felt the passion of that statement travel through her body, and then it dawned on her. "Toly Clayton. Your brother is the tie-roping state champion!"

Something flickered in the depths of his gray eyes. "That's right. Toly's my baby brother."

"Philipsburg is on the pro rodeo circuit for July 2. I'm a big fan of his. Wouldn't it be something if he wins the championship in December?"

"That's his dream."

"We'll be rooting for him."

"Who's we?"

"My parents and I."

His half smile turned her heart over. "He's the famous one in our family."

"How many siblings do you have?"

"Three brothers."

"What are your other brothers' names?"

"Roce and Eli."

"Those are good English names."

He nodded. "Wymon and Elias Clayton, two brothers who were immigrants from Lancashire, England, came to Montana in the mid-1800s. The names got handed down."

"No girls in your family?"

Another smile broke the corner of his compelling mouth. "My brother Eli got married recently. Now my mother has a daughter-in-law and a granddaughter. That helps."

So the other three brothers weren't married. That included the gorgeous male seated across from her.

He finished off another roll. "What about you? Do you have siblings?"

"No. My parents had almost given up on having children when I came along. You're lucky to have come from a big family."

"It has its moments, but I wouldn't trade any one of them." She heard love in his voice before he said, "If you're through eating, I'll walk you back. I know you're anxious to find out how Mr. Farnsworth is doing."

Of course she was worried, but she'd also enjoyed talking to Wymon and suffered more guilt for admitting it to herself. "I hope they don't find anything else wrong with him."

"He seemed to be all right, and the concussion will heal. As for you, from where I'm sitting, no one would guess that a few hours ago you barely escaped a plane crash."

"This whole day has been surreal."

"I can only imagine. After your experience, you're going to feel aches and pains and need rest, even if you're fighting it now."

"I'm sure you're right."

They got up and went back to the ER. He entered the cubicle with her. "Why don't you lie on top of the bed and relax? I'll see what I can find out about Mr. Farnsworth."

She watched him disappear. The man had a way of being in charge without doing anything overt. He was intrinsically kind. Solid. She knew she could trust him. He was a person she imagined other people leaned on. *And you're thinking about him* way *too much.*

Suddenly exhausted, Jasmine got on the bed and lay down on her side. Poor Rob. This day had turned into a nightmare for him. The only kind of comfort he would want was to hear that she would marry him.

Tears trickled from her eyes because she couldn't tell him something she didn't feel. Restless, she turned on her other side.

If only she'd acted on her worry that he was getting way too serious. She should have found an excuse not to go away with him. The thought of hurting him at all was bad enough. But to hurt him right before their accident made everything so much worse. How was she going to get out of that rally she'd promised to attend with him?

Tears of guilt overtaking her, she buried her face in the pillow.

When Wymon returned to the cubicle, he could hear that Jasmine was crying. He stood outside the curtain until her sobs subsided. When he pulled it open, he could tell she'd fallen asleep. Good. It was what she needed. In fact, he was convinced she ought to be given a room for the night.

Before he drove back to the ranch, he asked to

speak to Dr. Turner and waited in the lounge outside the doors of the ER until he showed up ten minutes later.

Wymon got to his feet. "I'm going home, but before leaving I wanted to suggest that Ms. Telford be
given a room. She ate a good lunch, but went right
back to her bed after. I have no idea if or when her
parents are going to show up."

"I already planned to keep her overnight after I
went in to check on her and found her asleep," Dr.
Turner told him.

"Perfect. How is Mr. Farnsworth?"

"I haven't talked to the neurologist since the CAT
scan, but I trust I'll hear from him soon. You've done
everything you can do here, Wymon, and you need
some downtime to relax, too. Leave your name and
cell phone number with the receptionist in triage so
we can reach you if needed."

With a nod, he did as the doctor suggested before
going out to his truck. Then he drove back to the
ranch, passing the main ranch house and Eli's. A little
farther down the road was Luis and Solana's home.

Luis had come to work for Wymon's father years
earlier. With his dad's death just a year and a half
ago, Wymon and his brothers relied on Luis, who
was the best ranch foreman of anyone around. Solana, the housekeeper at the main ranch house where
his mother lived, had become a permanent fixture in
the Clayton household.

Wymon's place was farthest up the road. After
parking his truck next to the Audi at the side of his

log cabin-style house, he headed for the kitchen. Once he'd pulled a cold beer from the fridge, he took the stairs two at a time to the loft.

When he'd moved into the two-bedroom house six years ago at the age of twenty-two, it was only one story. Since then he'd slowly had renovations done and it was now a two-story house with a bedroom, bath and loft on the second floor.

He loved sleeping upstairs in his modern bedroom where he could look out at the stars and the Sapphire Mountains while he lay in bed. The floor-to-ceiling windows made him feel as if he was sleeping outside.

The scenery drew him like a magnet. He took the lid off the bottle and drank half of it while he looked out at the vista that now included one crumpled blue-and-white Cessna. The sight of Jasmine Telford courageously trying to pull the pilot out of the cockpit would never leave him. Neither would the picture of her lying on the hospital bed, looking so beautiful. Those green eyes of hers had mesmerized him.

Over the last few hours he'd had time to put the pieces together. The two crash victims had been on their way to Seattle, no doubt in love and eager to get away for a vacation. With both of them coming from political backgrounds, they were well matched and well heeled. Particularly Robert Farnsworth, whose father and grandfather had made millions in oil.

She'd make a gorgeous wife for the aggressive Montana Representative. Give the man another eight to ten years and Wymon figured he'd have aspirations for something bigger in the future.

Was she as ambitious? Did she look forward to a life with him? Possibly in Washington, DC? Wining and dining with other One Percenters for the rest of their lives?

Wymon wished he didn't want to know the answer to that question. He had to think back to his bull-riding days in high school to remember what it was like to be this attracted to a woman on sight.

Sheila Rogers, a popular, attractive girl from his high school, had been the daughter of a local rancher. Wymon had fallen hard for her. They'd planned to get married after college. But she'd enrolled in a study-abroad program in Italy and met a guy there who was on location making a Hollywood movie.

When she returned home she had stars in her eyes. She wasn't the same girl who'd sobbed in his arms before leaving for Europe and had promised to email him every day and send pictures.

Sheila had broken up with Wymon, telling him she couldn't imagine living on a ranch with him for the rest of her life. He knew she hadn't intended to be cruel about it, just honest, but it had hurt him badly. Her honesty had broken his heart, but it also taught him a lesson. Before he knew it, Sheila had married the guy she met in Italy and moved to California, excited to embrace a brand-new way of life.

Since then he'd dated his fair share of women. But he didn't like it that after all this time he once again found himself attracted to a woman who'd purposely put herself in a position to embrace an exciting life far away from Montana with a man of prominence and means.

Though Wymon didn't have an idea of the perfect woman, he hoped one day to meet someone who wanted the same basic things from life that he did. So far she hadn't come along. And if she never did?

He wheeled around and bounded back down the stairs, setting the half-empty bottle on the kitchen counter before leaving the house. Needing to channel his frustration, he raced up to the barn and saddled his quarter horse.

"Let's get out of here, Titus. We both need a workout," he said and headed off into the mountains to clear his head.

# Chapter Three

By midafternoon Jasmine's parents had arrived at the hospital. She told them everything that had happened, leaving out the part about Rob proposing to her. Dr. Turner had transferred her to a room on the second floor and ordered her to rest. Her folks would be coming back in the morning to pick her up and drive her back to Philipsburg.

At six that evening, Rob's parents showed up and asked her to walk with them to his room, which was four doors down the hall. Jasmine had met them on several occasions and was comfortable being in their company.

While the three of them congregated around Rob, their dinners were brought in and they ate. His folks shed tears and were overjoyed that they'd both survived the crash. She doubted Rob had told them about what had happened in the cockpit before the hawk had flown into the propeller.

They treated her as if she'd be a member of their family one day soon, adding to her consternation. Rob lay there with his head bandaged. A plastic surgeon had put in the three stitches needed. They'd given him pain medication after monitoring his condition all afternoon.

Hard as it was, Jasmine had to pretend everything was all right between them in front of his parents. "Rob? How are you feeling?" she asked him.

"Rocky—dizzy—" The way he stared at her between narrowed lids made it clear to her that he wanted to say, *How the hell do you think I feel after you rejected me?*

Guilt stabbed at her. "I'm so sorry you were hurt. Just remember that you saved our lives because of the miraculous way you landed the plane. What will happen to it now?"

"I'll take care of it," his father answered for him. "We just want him to get well and back on track as fast as possible for the big rally in three weeks."

You couldn't keep a Farnsworth down. "I want that for you, too."

Rob grimaced at her remark. She knew how much emotional pain he was in. But she was in pain, too, because she knew in her heart she wouldn't be changing her mind about him. He was a good man, but marriage to him wouldn't work.

His mother turned to her. "Tell us about Mr. Clayton—I hear he came to your rescue after the crash landing."

Jasmine didn't dare look at Rob, knowing both men were political foes over the grizzly issue. "I undid the latch the way Rob told me to and tried to pull him out of the cockpit, but he was trapped. That's when Mr. Clayton saw us. He carried me to the trees, then ran back to help Rob."

"What an amazing coincidence that he would be there at that precise moment," Rob's mother murmured.

"I know. It was like he appeared out of the blue. Apparently he'd seen the plane go down and called 911. After he lifted Rob from the wreckage, he brought him over by me and gave him CPR. He was amazing. While I was sitting there in a daze, he brought me a cola and covered us with blankets. It wasn't long after that that the paramedics arrived."

Mr. Farnsworth cleared his throat. "We'll have to thank him for helping save your lives."

Jasmine noticed Rob didn't say anything. She decided to leave it to his parents to ask the doctor how to get in touch with Wymon Clayton. Just the thought of him made her heart race, followed by more guilt that she would still be thinking about him.

She didn't want to be reminded of the way it felt when he'd placed the blanket around her shoulders at the crash site. When his chin had brushed her hair and she'd smelled the soap he used in the shower, she'd felt his presence in every atom of her body.

Fearing this conversation was bothering Rob, she didn't dare volunteer any more information about the man who'd rescued them. Their son didn't need to know that they'd eaten lunch together in the hospital cafeteria and had talked about their families. Already, she was thinking ahead to the rodeo next weekend in Philipsburg, wondering if he'd be there. Forbidden thoughts she shouldn't be having continued to bombard her.

A nurse came in the room to check Rob's vital signs. She told them visiting hours were over and that Jasmine needed to get back to her room to be checked. Jasmine was so relieved for the interruption, she could have cried. This was one time Rob couldn't object.

She said good-night to his parents and squeezed Rob's hand. "Get a good sleep. I'll call you on the phone tomorrow after my parents drive me home." He gave her a wounded stare before she left the room and hurried down the hall.

After getting ready for bed, Jasmine lay there with the TV on, not watching anything. Because she'd slept all afternoon, she was wide-awake now. At ten o'clock the news came on.

Their accident was the lead story. To her relief there were no pictures, just the statement that Representative Robert Farnsworth and a companion had survived a crash in the Sapphires, with Mr. Farnsworth suffering a concussion. More news to come later.

She imagined Rob's campaign manager, Buzz Hendricks, had made certain to keep the details to a minimum. If news had leaked out that it was Wymon Clayton of all people who'd come to the rescue, that wouldn't have been the kind of information Rob would care to have taking the spotlight away from him.

With her thoughts less than charitable, she turned

off the TV, refusing to think any more about it tonight. Every time someone came in her room, she secretly hoped it might be the charismatic rancher just wanting to check up on her. But why would he do that when he knew she'd been on her way to Seattle with Rob? She was delusional to think he'd be interested in her.

What a pathetic fool she was to wish that he might want to see her again. Wymon was so attractive, he could have any woman he wanted and was probably living with one right now. During their conversation earlier, neither of them had talked about their personal lives. Those feelings of hers were all one-sided, and she needed to put them away.

Before she finally went to sleep, she came to a conclusion. In a few days when Rob was well, she would tell him emphatically that she couldn't envision a life with him. They had different temperaments, and it was better that they stop seeing each other.

She couldn't possibly go to the rally with him feeling the way she did. Even if she'd promised him several weeks ago, surely he couldn't want her there now that she'd turned down his proposal.

Jasmine did like him for many reasons, but it wasn't love. He deserved to find a woman who adored him heart and soul, who was compatible with him and wanted everything he had to offer.

In the morning, Dr. Turner did his rounds and released her, pronouncing her fit and ready to go home. Before he left the room she had a question to ask him.

"Would you by any chance know the directions to

the Clayton ranch business office? Since I'm here in Stevensville, now would be the perfect time to drive there and thank Mr. Clayton in person for all he did for me and Rob yesterday."

"That's easy. Travel five miles out on Highway 93. The ranch is clearly marked on the right. You'll find the main ranch house about a mile up the road."

"Thank you so much."

"You bet."

"I have one more question. Do you know of a store here that carries Western gear and blankets, that sort of thing?"

"Sure. Frost's Western Saddlery on Main Street."

"Wonderful. Thanks again."

"Best of luck to you and Representative Farns-worth."

One of the orderlies wheeled her out of the hospital to the car where her parents were waiting. She thanked him and hugged her parents. Once she'd gotten in back and her dad had put her bag in the trunk, she leaned forward.

"If you don't mind, I want to buy a gift for Mr. Clayton and take it to him before we drive home."

Her mom turned around. "What did you have in mind?"

"A saddle blanket. He used some blankets from his truck to keep us from going into shock. I think it would be a nice reminder."

"I think that's a lovely idea."

"Dr. Turner said I could find one at Frost's Western Saddlery on Main Street."

Her dad nodded, and he drove there, parking in front.

"I won't be long," she told her parents as she hurried into the store and approached the middle-aged man who asked if he could help her.

"I'm looking for a Nez Perce saddle blanket," she said. She had one herself and loved it.

"I have several. Come over this way." The man led her to another part of the store where he brought out four different samples. Her eye was drawn to a black-and-beige blanket with a distinctive indigenous design. For some reason she could see Mr. Clayton using it.

"I like this one."

"That's an excellent choice. It's a heavy-duty wool blanket. Perfect for our Montana weather, especially in the winter."

"How much is it?"

"Two hundred dollars."

There wasn't enough money in the world to pay Wymon back for what he'd done for her and Rob. "I'll take it. Could you wrap it as a gift for a man?"

"Of course."

She handed him her credit card and walked around the shop. When she saw a beautiful, long-sleeved ivory Western blouse with snap closures, she lifted it off the rack. Delighted to discover it was her size, she rushed over to the counter with it. "I'd like this, too, but it doesn't need to be wrapped."

Before long the salesman had bagged her purchases and handed her card back to her. "Come and visit us again," he said.

"I will. Thank you."

She hurried outside to her family. "The Clayton Ranch is only five miles from here. The doctor gave me directions. Mr. Clayton might not be in his office, but it doesn't matter. I'd just like to drop this off to let him know how much I appreciate what he did for us."

"We'd like to thank him ourselves," her dad said. "Tell me the directions."

It wasn't long before they arrived at the ranch with its arch of antlers welcoming them to the property. They drove up the road. The setting was like something out of a storybook with the gorgeous mountains in the background. Around a curve sat a fabulous two-story ranch house that had to have been built before the turn of the last century.

They pulled up to the office parking area. "I'll run in and see if he's there. If he is, I'll phone you to come in. Otherwise I'll just leave my gift."

She pulled the wrapped package out of its sack and walked up on the porch. There was a sign to ring the bell. After a minute, a pretty Hispanic woman opened the door. "Yes?"

"I've come to see Mr. Clayton. Is he here?"

"He's just leaving. Did you have an appointment?"

"No."

"May I tell him who's calling?"

"Jasmine Telford."

"Come in." Jasmine followed her through the entry hall to the living room. "Wait here. I'll get him."

Jasmine looked around the beautifully decorated

room. It was straight out of the pages of *True West* magazine.

*"Ms. Telford?"*

Wymon's deep voice set her heart racing before she turned around to see the handsome rancher enter the room, wearing his cowboy hat. She'd been told she'd caught him on his way out. It was pure luck that he was still there.

"I know I'm the last person you ever expected to see again, and I don't want to hold you up. But I was just released from the hospital and wanted to thank you again before I left for Philipsburg. This is for you," she said, handing him the gift.

He took it from her. "You shouldn't be giving me anything."

She smiled. "Let's agree not to argue about it. You and I both know what you did. Please, accept this with my heartfelt gratitude."

Their eyes held for a moment before he took off the wrapping. When he let the blanket unfold, she knew she'd picked the right one for him. She could see the pleasure in his silvery eyes.

"You have excellent taste. Thank you."

"You're welcome. Well, I'd better be going."

He studied her face. "Give Mr. Farnsworth my best. I'm sure you'll both be happy to get home and put that plane crash behind you."

It already *was* behind her. She'd hoped Mr. Clayton would want to talk to her for a few more minutes, but he was on his way out with other things on his mind. Worse, he assumed she and Rob were still a couple.

Mr. Clayton didn't know anything about her relationship with Rob. At this point she didn't dare blurt out that they wouldn't be seeing each other anymore. As if Mr. Clayton cared…

"Thanks again," she said and gave him a wave before exiting the door. Once in the car she told her parents she'd given him the gift. "He's a busy man and was on his way out. That's why I didn't invite you in to meet him."

Her mom smiled at her. "I'm sure he appreciated the gift."

"I think he did. Thanks for bringing me here."

On the way back to Philipsburg she unloaded about Rob. "Right before the crash he asked me to marry him, but I had to turn him down. Right after I told him that, the hawk hit the propeller. It was awful!"

Her emotions got the best of her, and tears started running down her cheeks.

"Oh, darling," her mother said sympathetically, turning around in her seat.

"Sorry. I really don't want to think about it anymore. As for Rob, I do like him a lot, but I'm not in love with him. I know he'll meet someone someday who wants the same things in life and will jump at the chance to be his wife. I'm just not that person."

"It's better you found out now, honey," her mother said.

"I didn't know how strongly I felt until we took off

in his new plane. He couldn't stop talking about his work. I thought we were going on a mini vacation to get away from his deadlines, but he told me he had business in Seattle. That's when I realized his work is like an obsession with him."

"Some people are made that way," her father stated.

"Some people aren't! I'm afraid I'm one of those." Her dad laughed and she continued, "All I know is, I *can't* live with his energy and won't be attending his rally. He's hoping I'll change my mind, but I won't. I know you two like him a lot and are probably disappointed."

Her mother looked back at her. "You're the one who has to live with him. If he isn't your be-all, end-all, then the last thing we'd want is to condemn you to an unhappy marriage. One day the right man will show up when you least expect it."

With that statement, Jasmine felt chills run up and down her spine.

WYMON STOOD THERE holding the blanket in his hands. How he wished Jasmine Telford hadn't come by the ranch house just now! If he hadn't stopped to eat breakfast first, he would have missed her. To see her again this soon hadn't given him enough time to get over his feelings for her. Now *this*!

He examined the elegant blanket she'd handpicked for him. His gut told him this hadn't been Representative Farnsworth's idea.

Wymon figured the other man didn't have a clue

that she'd bought him a present, certainly not one that suited him so perfectly. Her parents must have driven her to the ranch before taking her home because her boyfriend was still in the hospital recovering from his concussion.

After wadding up the wrapping paper, Wymon left through the front door and headed for his truck. He put the blanket and paper on the seat next to him and drove to the pasture to join the stockmen. But the whole way there he was haunted by the woman who'd come to mean so much to him in such a short time. He could feel the depth of her gratitude down to his bones. *Damn, damn, damn.*

For the rest of the week he divided his time between ranch work and his talks with various members of the coalition. To his chagrin, no matter how hard he worked, Jasmine Telford kept invading his thoughts until he was just about driven out of his mind.

A big mistake was putting the new blanket on Titus. Now there was a connection with her he could feel every time he mounted his horse. It reminded him of putting one of his blankets around her at the crash site. Had that been the reason she'd chosen this particular gift for him? Somehow he had to throw this off, but heaven help him, he didn't know how.

THE DAY OF the rodeo, Wymon had ranch business in Missoula and was going to be late if he didn't hurry. When he got in his truck, he reached behind the visor before realizing the really good sunglasses he used for driving long distances weren't there.

Where had they gone?

He didn't have time to stop in town for another pair and would have to purchase new ones later.

After the morning meeting with the president of the Cattlemen's Association, he swung by the veterinary hospital. Roce was waiting for him so they could drive together for the hour-and-a-half trip to Philipsburg to meet up with Toly for the rodeo.

"What happened at the meeting?"

"The committee wants to put up my name as president elect of the association."

"Congratulations, bro."

"Save it, Roce. I told them no."

"Why? You'd be a breath of fresh air."

He shook his head. "Since the grizzly decision was put off a month, I need this time to rally more support and donors before our next meeting with the governor. I don't have time to think about the Cattlemen's Association right now."

"Can't you do both? Eli is running things on the ranch to free you up."

"Our brother does the work of ten men, but that's not it. I can't sink my teeth into business while—"

"While you're still trying to win over more supporters," Roce broke in. "I know. Representative Farnsworth has been vicious in his attacks against your coalition. I'm upset about it, too. But something else is bothering you. What is it?"

"What do you mean?"

"I don't know exactly. Even Mom noticed you were different at Sunday dinner when we learned you saw that plane crash and helped the victims. You're a real hero, bro."

Wymon scoffed. "I just happened to be there at the right moment."

"True, but it's pretty amazing that you happened to rescue Farnsworth, of all people. To think he's been one of the most outspoken voices against the grizzly reintroduction program. You must have been shocked to discover he was the pilot."

"I believe it was an even bigger shock for him to discover that *I* was the first responder, but he and his parents acted grateful on the phone to me."

He felt his brother's eyes on him. "Even though I'm a veterinarian, I know a little about the human psyche. What's going on with you emotionally? Something has upset you."

Roce didn't miss much.

"Let's just say that during the experience, I was revisited by a ghost from the past."

"Something to do with Dad?"

"No."

"Look—if you need to talk about it, I'm a good listener."

"You're the best."

"Then spill!"

Caught at a vulnerable moment he blurted the truth. "The woman with him got to me."

"Ah." There was a wealth of understanding in Roce's tone. "In other words, you've found yourself smitten. Did she remind you of Sheila?" Roce was so quick on the draw, it was scary.

"Not in looks. What I'm saying is that meeting her was like being served a dose of déjà-vu. How is it that once again I'm attracted to a woman who wants to marry a guy who'll give her a life of glamor and excitement? Flyover country doesn't compete with Washington, DC or Hollywood."

Roce chuckled. "You can't make a statement like that on the strength of two women out of the millions in the universe."

Wymon flashed him a grudging smile. "You ought to know. How many women have you gone through by now? Forty? Fifty?"

"You mean in a year?"

Wymon shook his head. Their mother despaired of either of them ever settling down.

"A hell of a lot more that that!"

Driving with Roce had been good for him.

"I take it the woman was a goddess?"

Laughter broke from Wymon. "You know what they say about beauty. It's in the eye of the beholder."

"My gut tells me she had to be pretty incredible to put you in this condition. What was her name?"

"Jasmine Telford, but it doesn't matter. I don't want to talk about her."

"How much time did you actually spend with her?"

"A couple of hours. When the doctor sent her to a private room, I left. That's the end of the story. Thanks for listening."

He could have told him she'd come by the ranch last Saturday to give him the saddle blanket, but talking about it would only make matters worse. She wasn't available. Somehow he had to snap out of it.

"Anytime."

Wymon's pulse picked up speed as he drove them through town where Jasmine lived. They stopped to pick up hamburgers and shakes before heading to the arena where the rodeo would be taking place. Roce didn't know Jasmine was from Philipsburg, or that she might be at the rodeo with her lover who had to be recovered by now.

If Wymon hadn't promised Toly he'd be there, he would never have come. Eli's little girl was sick. He and Brianna hadn't been able to make it this time around. Neither had their mother, who'd come down with the same cold.

It was up to Wymon and Roce to support their little brother. They'd all done bull riding and tie-roping in their teens and knew what it meant to see a family member in the stands cheering them on.

After parking the truck, they walked over to the area reserved for the horse trailers and found Toly's big silver-and-black rig. Roce knocked on the door. When Toly opened it, Wymon grinned. "Dinner has arrived," he announced.

"Man, I thought you'd never get here. We're starving!"

They went inside and sat around with him and his partner, Mills, while they ate and talked shop about the competition for tonight's rodeo. Toly wanted to hear about the plane rescue. Wymon gave him a superficial report, and then the four of them walked over to the pens to check out the livestock.

After a while they moved to the area where the horses were stalled. Roce gave both their horses a thorough exam. Once he declared them healthy and ready to go, it was almost time for the parade to start.

Wymon and Roce wished the guys luck, then found seats down in front to enjoy the rodeo. Neither of them had been to Philipsburg in several years. Roce commented that the grounds had been improved with new bucking chutes and more concessions. But Wymon had other things on his mind.

He wondered if the woman who'd caused him to lose sleep over the last week had come to the rodeo. Knowing he had to be here for Toly and might see her was the reason for Wymon's agitation.

From time to time he looked around the huge crowd but didn't see her or Rob Farnsworth. That was good. Once Toly's event was over, he and Roce would take off for Missoula. Then Wymon could drive back to the ranch and put all this behind him.

The night proved to be a stunning success for Toly and Mills who captured another gold buckle. After hugs and congratulations behind the scenes with no sign of Ms. Telford being anywhere around, Wymon and Roce got back in the truck and headed for Missoula. Alternate sensations of relief and disappointment washed over him.

Once he'd dropped off Roce at his condo in Missoula, he took off for home. No sooner had he left the city limits than his cell rang. He checked the caller ID and clicked on.

"Toly? I didn't expect to hear from you tonight. I thought you'd be out celebrating. What's wrong?"

"Nothing at all. When I finally got back to the trailer, there was a visitor waiting for me. She was hoping to see you, but you and Roce were long gone. I could tell by her expression that she was disappointed."

Wymon's hand tightened on the phone. "She?" He knew full well who his brother meant.

"Yeah. Jasmine Telford, the woman you helped at the crash site. I thought you'd want to know she teared up when she told me what you did for them. I never saw anyone so grateful."

He struggled for breath. "Was Representative Farnsworth with her tonight?"

"No. She was alone. Mills already has a horrible crush on her. We found out she lives here in Philipsburg. He already has plans to call her."

"I'm afraid she's spoken for."

"He said he didn't see a ring and figures all's fair…"

A groan escaped Wymon.

"Hey, bro—are you still there?"

"Yes."

"It's just like my big brother never to give anything away—like the fact that this woman you saved is such a hottie! I'd go after her myself, but it might be the end of Mills and me."

"I thought you and Olivia were together."

"You thought wrong." Whatever was going on with Toly, he wasn't about to give anything away, either. They weren't brothers for nothing.

"Even when you two win at nationals in December, you should warn Mills she's after the limelight only a politician like Representative Farnsworth can offer."

"Try telling that to my partner. Hey—I have friends waiting and need to go. One more thing before we hang up. She said that when her parents drove her home, she found a pair of men's expensive sunglasses in her suitcase. They're aviator Ray-Bans, gunmetal brown."

He remembered taking them off in the cubicle. So that was where they'd disappeared to.

"She thinks they were somehow put in her bag when she was transferred to a private room and thought they might be yours. She brought them with her and will be happy to send them to you."

He couldn't believe it. "They're definitely mine. I was looking for them this morning. Thanks for passing that along. I'll get in touch with her. Good luck at your next rodeo. Where will it be?"

"In North Dakota, too far for you to come. It meant a lot to see you there tonight."

"We wouldn't have missed it. Take care. Drive safely."

"You, too. Give Mom a hug."

"Will do."

By the time he reached his house, Wymon's heart had slowed down to a rate that wasn't quite off the charts. Out of all the questions he wanted answered, one stood out above the others. After the event, why had Jasmine sought out his brother when she could have phoned the Clayton ranch instead and left a message?

If Wymon were in her lover's shoes, he wouldn't have liked learning that she'd gone out of her way to make contact with another man.

When he realized how unreasonable, even over the top, that sounded, he levered himself from the cab and strode swiftly toward the house.

*You're a fool, Clayton, because, despite everything, you were thrilled when she came to the ranch to give you that blanket. You know you're dying to see her again.*

At 8:30 a.m., Jasmine's phone rang. She got a sick feeling that it was Rob again. Sure enough, when she checked, it was his caller ID. The only way out of this was to end it for good. She clicked on. "Hi, Rob."

"Jasmine—I'm glad you're awake and picked up. I've asked Buzz to clear my calendar so we can spend the day together. This will be our first chance to talk face-to-face since the hospital."

He'd phoned her every day, insisting she needed to give their relationship more time because he wasn't taking no for an answer. She hadn't wanted to be unkind to him while he was recovering, but this situation couldn't go on any longer.

"I'm sure you're still not well enough to drive here from Helena."

"What are you talking about? My own doctor checked me out two days ago and said I was good as new. I was in meetings all day yesterday. Now I'm free to be with you. We'll grab lunch at the Regency House. Buzz made reservations for us at twelve."

Her hand tightened on the phone while she girded up her courage to be firm in a way he couldn't misunderstand. "I don't want you to come, Rob. We've talked about this every day. I can't marry you because I don't love you the way you need to be loved." She bit her lip. "I'm sorry. Let's not hurt each other anymore by doing this. Both of us survived the crash and are alive and well. Can't we at least part as friends?"

She heard his sharp intake of breath. "I don't believe you can just shut us down like this. You don't know the dreams I've had about us and the life we're going to have. I'm in love with you. I want to spend my life with you and refuse to believe you're not giving us a chance."

Jasmine didn't doubt his feelings for her. But more and more she understood that he always needed to win. He wouldn't accept that this was one race he'd already lost, great as he was. "I never meant to hurt you, Rob, and now I have to go."

"Jasmine? Don't you dare hang up on me!"

His flare of temper appeared now and again when he was interviewed by the local press, but this was the first time she'd known it to be directed at her. She realized it was his pain talking and forgave him for it, but this had to be the end. "Then what should I do? There's nothing more to say."

"What's happened to you?"

After taking a deep breath she said, "It's a case of what *hasn't* happened to me. I didn't fall in love with you. I know that's painful to hear, and I'm so sorry. Please, know how much I've enjoyed all our times together. We share some wonderful memories, and I wish you nothing but the very best. Goodbye, Rob."

Closing her eyes tightly she clicked off, relieved this moment was over. Relieved her relationship with him was truly over.

No sooner had she'd gotten off the phone with Rob than it rang again. Fearing he still refused to give up, she glanced at the caller ID. When she saw the name, her breath caught before she picked up. She'd been hoping to hear from Wymon before the day was out.

"Mr. Clayton?"

"Good morning, Ms. Telford. I hope it isn't too early to call."

"Not at all."

"My brother phoned me while I was on my way home last night and told me you have my sunglasses."

"Yes! I was so surprised when I saw them while I was unpacking. The orderly who transferred me to my room must have put them in there. They looked expensive."

"I'll admit I'm glad they've been found."

"I decided they must be yours and thought I'd see you at the rodeo. We must have just missed each other."

"My brother and I had to leave immediately after

Toly's event. He had to get back to the animal hospital in Missoula because he was on call."

"I take it he's a vet."

"One of the best. Tell me—would you be home later today? If so, I'll come by for them."

Her hand went to her throat. "Aren't you in Stevensville?"

"It's only a two-hour drive and will be worth it. Is there a time that's convenient for you?"

She looked at her watch, so thrilled she could hardly stand it. It was five after nine. "Anytime. I'm not going anywhere today."

"You don't work on weekends?"

"No. My job is a Monday through Friday position."

"What do you do?"

"I'm an administrator for the Montana 4-H Foundation through Montana State University."

"I thought you were an attorney. Here I was imagining you working day and night on some case."

Jasmine rolled her eyes. "Perish the thought."

"I heard otherwise. My mistake for eavesdropping on the paramedics' private conversation. One of them got his facts wrong." She laughed and he said, "Give me some specifics about what you do."

She liked it that he sounded interested. "Oh, lots of things. I help raise private funds and manage financial resources. I partner with the extension division to fund educational opportunities for youth."

"What made you go into that?"

"My mom. She got into 4-H years ago and volunteered. As soon as I could sit on a pony, she had me involved, and I never outgrew it."

"I like that image of you. After I reach Philipsburg, I hope you'll agree to go to lunch with me. I need to pick your brains."

She chuckled. "What do you mean?"

"Finding funds for the bill I'm anxious to get picked up is my main objective for the foreseeable future. Hope you don't mind if I avail myself of your expertise. I'll try to be there by twelve thirty so we'll have plenty of time to talk. Does that sound good to you?"

If he only knew... "More than good, but only if I pay."

"No. After that blanket you gave me and my horse, it's my turn. Titus is crazy about the design and says thank you."

That meant Wymon liked it, too. "Tell him he's very welcome."

"Give me your address."

After they'd exchanged information, he said, "See you then."

The minute she hung up, she slid out of bed and ran to the bathroom to shower and wash her hair. After drying it, she put on her favorite short-sleeved denim shirt dress with a narrow tan braided belt, a casual look and perfect for eating out. Her leather sandal wedges matched the belt.

She hadn't fooled the rancher. He knew she'd approached his brother after the rodeo on purpose, hoping for today's outcome. Jasmine surprised herself that she'd been daring enough to do something her unmarried friends did all the time.

They saw no sin in letting a man know you were interested in him. But this was the second time for her to take the initiative—the first time by stopping at his ranch to give him a present. He brought out feelings in her that had made her do something unprecedented where a man was concerned.

After finding her and Rob together and knowing they were flying to Seattle, Mr. Clayton had to assume the two of them were a couple who might even be unofficially engaged. He hadn't asked personal questions. Under the unique circumstances of their meeting, he wasn't the type to make the first move even if he were interested in her. It had been up to Jasmine.

Now, to her joy, she had butterflies because he was driving all the way to see her in order to get his glasses. He hadn't asked her to mail them. This was her first clue that he wanted to see her again.

She was thankful her parents wouldn't be getting home from Helena before evening. They would question why the rancher had come to Philipsburg on such a flimsy pretext. More questions would follow when they learned that she'd agreed to go out to lunch with him.

Her dad, particularly, would wonder how his daughter could have decided to go away with Rob for the weekend, and within a week of breaking up with him had started seeing another man.

Poor Rob. After the crash she hadn't wanted to

say or do anything to hinder his recovery. No one was more thankful than Jasmine that his concussion hadn't been more serious, and now he was well. But trying to soft-pedal her rejection before today hadn't convinced him she meant it. After their conversation this morning, he had to know in his heart that it was over. They both needed to move on.

Now here she was getting ready to go out to lunch with the awesome rancher. Looking at it from what she expected was her father's perspective, Jasmine had to question her own sanity. But she'd never loved Rob, and she hadn't felt the same since the moment the tall, dark stranger had appeared seemingly out of nowhere to help her pull him from the cockpit.

## Chapter Four

The doorbell rang as Jasmine was putting on lipstick.
Somehow she had to find a way to calm down before
she answered it. She reached for her purse containing
the sunglasses and walked through the house. How
embarrassing to sound out of breath as she opened
the door to the head of the Clayton ranch.

Beneath his black Stetson, those silvery gray eyes
narrowed on her features, making her tremble. He
was wearing a charcoal Western shirt and tan Wran-
gler dress pants. The man looked amazing whatever
he had on.

She hung on to the door handle. "You got here fast."

A beguiling half smile appeared. "I'm afraid I've
racked up a few speeding tickets in my time."

"So have I," she confessed. "Would you like to
come in?"

"Maybe when I bring you home. Since it's a Sunday, I took the liberty of making a reservation at the
Silver Mill in case it's crowded."

"Ooh—then we shouldn't be late. It's a wonderful restaurant."

"I ate there some time ago and was determined to go back. Are you ready to leave?"

"I am." She shut and locked the door before he helped her get in his truck. The interior held the faint scent of the same soap she'd smelled on him a week ago. It brought back a memory so fresh, the accident could have just happened.

When he walked around and got behind the wheel, she opened her purse and handed him the sunglasses. He put them on and turned to her. No man anywhere would ever look as good to her as he did. "You've made my day in more ways than one, Ms. Telford."

*Tell me about it.* "Please, call me Jasmine."

"Before I do that, I need an answer to one question." She suspected what it was. "If you don't plan to tell Mr. Farnsworth you've been with me, then I'll walk you back to your house, and we won't be seeing each other again."

She'd sensed he was an honorable man. Now she knew it beyond all doubt. "Wymon—I hope you don't mind that I no longer think of you as Mr. Clayton. You of all people deserve an explanation. Rob and I are over and won't be seeing each other again."

She heard him suck in his breath. "Does he know that?"

"Yes. We've been talking since he got out of the hospital. I've dated him exclusively for three months and cared for him a great deal, but all along I've had my reservations. Just little things, but they added up. We have no future together. I—I hope that answers your question," she stammered.

"I appreciate your honesty, but he's not the kind of man to take no for an answer."

Jasmine eyed him curiously. "How do *you* know that?"

"Because I've been battling his politics for the last half a year."

She heard a world of emotion in that comment. "I know he's been battling *yours*," she said.

His jaw tightened. "He's not going to like it if he gets wind that you've gone out to lunch with me."

"I can't help that. He's going in one direction. I'm going in another. That's one of the major reasons we didn't work out. It's a fact of life that you put your own life in jeopardy by coming to our rescue. That kind of selflessness and courage is something I'll never forget. Though I gave you a gift, it still wasn't enough. I've wanted to see you again and tell you how grateful I am," she admitted.

"Jasmine—" his voice grated.

Her heart leaped to hear him say her name, but she was afraid, too. "But if you tell me you think I'm emotionally unstable because of the crash and don't know my own mind, then I'll get out of the truck right now, and we won't be seeing each other again."

A strange sound came out of him. He flung off his glasses, then leaned across and caught her softly rounded chin in his hand so she was forced to look him in the eyes. They'd darkened with emotion.

"When I witnessed the way you rose to the occasion to save his life and handle yourself at the crash site, I knew you were the most emotionally stable woman I would ever meet in my life!"

His words moved her deeply. "Thank you for saying that." She wanted him to kiss her. Oh, how much she wanted him to take her in his arms. But she didn't get her wish. He studied her for a long moment before letting her go. After putting his sunglasses back on, he started the engine and they left for the restaurant.

She was no longer the same woman who'd answered the front door. The earth had turned on its axis because Wymon Clayton had happened to her, and nothing would ever be the same again.

The day flew by while they ate and talked about their work—mostly hers because he badgered her with questions. Back at the house they walked to the barn where the family kept their horses. Jasmine made sure they all had water and hay. Wymon was such a great listener she didn't realize until later that he'd elicited more information from her than she'd ever told anyone.

He knew all about her love affair with horses and the loss of her mare Trixie. But she couldn't talk about how she'd died. Otherwise she knew she'd sob all over him. It had happened around the same time she'd met Rob, and it was still too painful. Since then she'd been planning to buy a new horse, but her heart hadn't been in it.

She had to stifle a moan when Wymon said he needed to leave. They walked out in front of the house to his truck. "I've been buying horses for the stockmen from my friend Jim Whitefeather in Missoula.

He's a horse trader I trust. Maybe he has one you'd be interested in. How would you like to spend next Saturday with me? We'll drive over to see him."

Jasmine struggled to remain calm. "You're willing to take that kind of time?"

"I'm allowed a day off once in a while," he quipped, "and I know what it's like to lose a favorite horse. The sooner you find a new one, the happier you'll be."

"You're so right." She didn't mean to keep comparing him to Rob. In truth there was no comparison, but Rob didn't understand how deeply she'd missed the horse who'd been like an extension of her. Wymon understood how hard it had been on her without even knowing the details.

"If you see one you want, I'll ask Roce to give it his seal of approval."

She was afraid to look at him for fear he'd see what was in her eyes. "Now I can't wait."

"Neither can I." His deep voice penetrated to her insides. "I'll give Jim a heads-up, then I'll call you and we'll make plans."

"I'll look forward to hearing from you. Thanks again for the delicious lunch and the talk. Next time it'll be your turn to talk nonstop to me. I want to hear about all the Clayton boys' adventures. When your brother wins the world championship in Las Vegas in December, I'll be able to tell my friend Annie that I have the inside scoop on him."

"Annie?"

"Yeah, she kind of has a little crush on Toly. Annie works for the university, too."

Low laughter rumbled out of him. It was such a good sound. "You don't want to hear about all of our adventures."

"Want to bet? I'm sure your brother Roce will be willing to tell me a few secrets about you if I ask him."

He levered himself in the cab with a smile and shut the door. "Talk to you soon."

After she watched him put on his cowboy hat and those sunglasses that were the reason today's outing even happened, he drove off, just before her parents turned into the driveway. If he'd stayed another minute longer, she would have been able to introduce them.

She followed their car up the driveway and hugged them after they got out. Her dad smiled at her. "Don't you look lovely! Where have you been? More importantly, with whom?"

"That was Wymon Clayton. He came to get those sunglasses I found."

"All the way from the Sapphire ranch, hmm?" Her mom smiled. "I wish he would come back so we could meet him and thank him in person for what he did to save your lives."

Her dad nodded. "I don't know if I told you. A long time ago he was one of the best bull riders around."

That little bit of news didn't surprise Jasmine one bit. "You'll get your chance to meet him next Saturday if you're home." She grabbed her mother's suitcase. They'd been gone overnight. Jasmine walked in the house with them. "He has a friend who sells horses and is going to help me pick one out."

Her dad brought up the rear. "So you're thinking about getting another one?"

"I'd always intended to, but—"

"But Rob took up a lot of your time," he interjected.

"Dating him helped me get my mind off her, yes. But in truth, I wasn't ready to think about another horse until now. Trixie meant the world to me."

He eyed her shrewdly. "It's really over with Rob, isn't it?"

"Yes. I shouldn't have dated him as long as I did. After a few dates, I knew something wasn't right, but at first I thought it was because I was so sad over Trixie. It was hard to sort out my feelings." She gave her dad a hug.

"So now they're sorted out?"

"Yes. How are things with the two of you?"

Her parents exchanged a glance. They had this way of looking at each other and saying a whole lot without speaking a word. She knew what they were thinking. *Our daughter has moved on. A new horse, a new man in her life.* And they'd be right!

Forty-five minutes later she was in the kitchen with her mom when her cell phone rang. She got the nagging fear that it was Rob, but to her joy she discovered it was the man who was already transforming her life. She picked up out of breath.

"Wymon?"

"Hi, Jasmine. If this is an inconvenient time to call, just tell me."

"Of course not."

"I just passed through Drummond and saw the signs for their Fourth of July celebration tomorrow. They're doing a later afternoon rodeo. It won't be pro rodeo, but it'll be fun, and it's followed by fireworks and a street dance. If you don't have plans, would you like to go with me?"

Jasmine didn't have to think. "I'd love it, but only if we meet there. It's too far for you to come all the way to Philipsburg."

"It's only twenty minutes more. That's nothing. I'll pick you up at three. See you then."

He clicked off before she was ready to let him go. Her mother smiled. "You remind me of me when I first met your father. I walked around in a perpetual daze."

Her mother still did.

"That's how it feels, Mom," Jasmine agreed, hoping against hope that this feeling would last forever.

WYMON COULD HEAR the announcer as he guided Jasmine through the crowd. "Welcome to the Drummond Rodeo, folks! Please, stand for the national anthem and parade."

He pulled Jasmine in front of him and held on to her shoulders while they sang. Then the parade began. "You smell marvelous," he whispered into her hair and felt a little tremor run through her.

"Thank you. So do you."

He squeezed her shoulders before letting her go. After the cheering subsided, the announcer spoke again. "All you cowboys and cowgirls—we've got events to tickle everyone's fancy. Two hours of chills, spills and thrills, so hold on to your britches."

The audience cheered because the bareback event had started. He guided her to some front row seats and noticed every guy in sight was checking her out. They could be forgiven for thinking she was the Drummond rodeo queen. In her Western fringe vest and white cowboy hat, Jasmine made it hard for him to keep his eyes and hands off her.

Normally he sat with his brothers to watch the rodeo. The thrill for him was sitting next to Jasmine who loved it and knew a lot about it. Next came the bull-riding event. When Danny Sloan, a local cowboy, got a score in the high seventies, Jasmine looked at Wymon.

"Oh, dear. Not the best numbers. I didn't know until my dad told me that you and your brothers were successful bull riders and tie ropers back in the day. He said you scored in the nineties a couple of times."

"That was ten years ago."

"Well I'm impressed and wish I'd seen you perform."

They watched an unknown win the tie-roping event. "Your brother's going to win in Las Vegas, I just know it," she said. "There's no one faster than Toly."

Jasmine was making his night in more ways than one. After the last event, he ushered her out of the arena to his truck. They drove to the area where the street dancing had been going on to a great live band.

Farther down was the park where the fireworks show was going to be held.

They got out and wandered around eating food from the various concessions. "This pig in a blanket is so good, but I'm too full and can't finish it, Wymon."

"Then throw it out and let's dance."

She did as he said before he pulled her into his arms. He swung her around a few times, and they ended up at the park where the fireworks were about to start.

He looked down at her flushed face. "Having a good time?"

"You know I am."

Before he could tell her how he felt, a sandy-haired man, probably in his thirties and dressed in a Western suit, came up to Jasmine and put a hand on her arm. "Jasmine! Imagine finding *you* here tonight!"

Wymon saw the light go out in her eyes. "Buzz? I was just going to say the same thing to you. I would have thought you'd be in Helena."

The fireworks show had started with a gigantic shower of red, white and blue stars.

"I had business here. Where's Rob? I assumed you'd come with him. Instead I find you with the head of the Clayton ranch, our opposition." He said it with a smile.

She turned to Wymon, looking nervous. "Wymon, this is Buzz Hendricks, Rob's manager."

Wymon recognized him and nodded. "Enjoying the rodeo?"

"I didn't get to see it."

At this point Jasmine spoke up. "Didn't Rob tell you that Mr. Clayton was the person who rescued us after the crash? If he hadn't seen the plane going down and called 911, I don't want to think what could have happened. Wymon gave Rob CPR because he'd been knocked unconscious and got his body out of the plane."

"I heard about it after the fact."

The way he'd said it, Wymon knew he'd been left in the dark. Interesting that Farnsworth hadn't told his manager any details. For obvious reasons, he hadn't wanted people to know Wymon had been involved. But for him not to tell his manager before the news broke did surprise him.

"It's nice to see you, Buzz. Now if you'll excuse us, we're going to sit on the bleachers to watch the fireworks."

Wymon knew the other man had a dozen questions, but he kept quiet. "See you again soon." He gave Wymon a penetrating stare before disappearing into the crowd.

Fireworks lit up the sky. Jasmine clung to his arm as he walked them over to one of the sets of bleachers. "I'm sorry that happened, Wymon."

"Since Rob chose not to tell his manager about me, it was only natural he was surprised to see you with anyone else."

"Buzz is going to have to get used to it."

"Are he and Rob close friends?"

"Yes. They went to high school together."

"Come on over here." He found a place on the end and pulled her up next to him. "I say let's enjoy the rest of the show."

They didn't talk about it the rest of the night. Once the finale had thrilled the crowd, they left for Philipsburg, and he saw her to the front door. "Thanks for going with me, Jasmine. I haven't had that much fun in a long time."

"Neither have I. I'm just sorry you have to drive all the way home now when it's so late."

"I like driving. It's the best time to talk to my friends on the committee and formulate new ideas. Get a good sleep. I'll see you in Missoula on Saturday, but expect a call from me before that."

She nodded and lifted pleading eyes to him. "Be safe on the road."

"Always," he replied before turning around and heading back to his truck, leaving her standing alone. The last thing he'd wanted to do was walk away. But as much as Wymon needed to kiss Jasmine goodnight, he held off and turned away, striding back to his truck. Once on the road he phoned Roce. He needed to unload. There was no better listener than his brother.

After Roce answered, he told him that he'd bumped into Rob Farnsworth's campaign manager and old school friend at the fireworks show in Drummond with Jasmine.

When he explained that Rob hadn't told his manager anything about the rescue, Roce let out a whistle. "Get ready for more fireworks, bro."

"Maybe."

"They were a couple until the crash. Now she's out with you? There's no maybe about it. Just be careful. Farnsworth has been after your hide, and this just adds fuel to that fire."

"You're right."

On the way home Wymon thought about what his brother had said, but there was nothing he could do about it. Already he was thinking about being with Jasmine again.

# *Chapter Five*

On Saturday morning after a shower and shave, he let himself into the main ranch house and found his mother in the kitchen enjoying breakfast with Luis and Solana. He walked over and gave her a kiss. "How are you feeling?"

"My cold is better. What brings you to the house this early when you were gone until late last night?"

"I have big plans today."

"Well, sit down and tell us about them while you eat."

"I can't. I don't have time."

She scrutinized him in a way only a mother could do. "That's obvious. You look excited about something."

"I'm meeting Jim in Missoula."

She cocked her head. "Still working on that bill before the next committee meeting with the governor?"

"Exactly. We've got some ideas and are anxious to find more backers to add weight to the campaign. But that's not my reason for going to see him today."

"Are you thinking of buying another horse?"

Luis's head lifted in surprise.

"No, Mom. I'm actually going to help someone else buy one."

"Ah. Anyone I know?"

"No."

"Does that mean you're not going to tell me?"

"It's not important. I only came by to make sure you were all right."

"This is the second Saturday you've taken off."

"Doesn't a man have the right?" he teased.

"Of course he has the right, but I haven't known you to exercise yours in a long, long time."

It was time to go. "Luis? I figure you and Eli are squared away for today. I'll see about the fencing in the north pasture tomorrow."

Luis nodded.

"In that case I can leave." He squeezed his mother's shoulder, then turned to Solana. "You're looking good."

As he wheeled away and headed for the front door he heard the housekeeper say, "He's never said that to me before. Something big is going on."

Wymon realized he'd made a mistake by dropping in to see his mother first. Now Solana suspected something unusual was going on, too. He'd always kept his private life private. Damn.

He jumped in his truck and headed for Missoula where he planned to meet Jasmine at the entrance to the Whitehorse Nez Perce horse ranch on the outskirts. Before yesterday they'd talked twice during the week about a possible purchase. In truth, he loved any reason to hear her voice. All week he'd been antsy waiting for today to roll around.

En route to the ranch, he phoned her. "Hi, Jasmine. Are you on your way?"

"I'm so glad you called, Wymon. I was just going to phone you."

He frowned. "Is anything wrong?"

"Not at all. I'm in the car driving too fast because I'm so excited to look at the horses."

Wymon's body relaxed. "I am, too," he said. But the horses weren't the only things he was excited about. "I talked to Jim earlier. He has seven horses for sale at the moment."

"What kinds?"

"To my recollection, a trail horse, two geldings, two mares, a filly and a colt."

"Ooh, I'd love a filly I can train, or the right mare."

"I'm positive you'll find one you like. I've been buying Nez Perce horses for several years."

"Why are they so special?"

"His line comes from the Ma'amin horses recovered from the Minam line of Chief Joseph's horses. Today there are approximately four thousand Nez Perce Indians left in the Pacific Northwest. In 1995 they started crossbreeding their own horse."

"I didn't realize that."

"It's a fascinating story. Jim's horses are a crossbreed of the Appaloosa and the Asian breed Akhal-Teke. According to him, the traits of endurance, substance and athleticism have been bred into them. He swears they're suited for every discipline."

"I have to admit it gives me chills to think I could own a horse with a history like that. What a great legacy from Chief Joseph."

If she'd only known it, every time she made remarks like that, she endeared herself to Wyman more and more.

"In my opinion, their intelligence and love for humans is extraordinary. We have a lot of horses on the ranch, but I have to tell you I've never found a breed easier to teach or more of a pleasure to live with."

"For you to say that has convinced me I can't go wrong if I find the one I want."

"Jim will give you some more reasons you need to get one. He'll tell you they're hardy and in good health. That makes them easy and economical to care for."

The two of them talked until they arrived at Jim's ranch. They drove up to the office where he introduced her to his friend. Jim walked them around to the huge corral where all the horses for sale were grazing.

"Oh, Wymon—look at that adorable brown-and-white marbled Appaloosa."

Jim smiled at him. "That's the only filly I have right now."

By the excitement in her voice, Jasmine had already made her choice anyway. "Can I go in and talk to her?"

Jim nodded. "She'll like that. She's very playful."

Wymon watched as she slipped into the corral and walked over to the filly. She'd been around horses all her life. That was apparent in the way she greeted the horse and touched it. Every so often he heard laughter and little sounds of delight come out of Jasmine.

She looked over at Wymon. "I love her. Do you think your brother could take a look at her? I plan to pay him."

"I'll call him right now," Wymon said.

Wymon had already told Jim what he'd planned to do so there wouldn't be any surprises. The whole time they waited for Roce, she stayed in the corral and handled the little filly as if the two of them had been friends for a long time.

"Ms. Telford has a way with horses."

"As I told you earlier, her last horse died three months ago. Obviously she's ready to be a parent again." They both chuckled before Jim grew more serious.

"I heard from Harry Walters. He wants a few of us from the committee to approach the Bennington Philanthropic Foundation."

Wymon nodded. "I've thought that would be a good route to go. With their name, their support would be a big coup for us. Let's talk later and make it happen."

While they stood talking, Roce came walking toward them with his bag. "I can see the horse you want me to check out."

"I saw you eyeing the potential buyer first," Wymon teased.

"Yup." He grinned at Wymon, then shook hands

with Jim. "Let's get that little beauty into the barn, so I can check her out."

Correction, Wymon mused. *Two* beauties.

All four of them accompanied the filly inside to her stall. After more introductions, Roce did his exam while Jasmine watched raptly. Wymon thought about how he preferred watching her. Jim had another prospective buyer to talk to, so he left the three of them alone for a time.

"This three-year-old has good ground manners and lets me touch her everywhere. Notice she even stays still for a stranger like me, another plus," Roce said. After a little while, he made a pronouncement. "Her hooves are clean. She's had floating maintenance. I'd say she's perfect. Jim has been an excellent trainer. You couldn't ask for more, unless you just find her too ugly."

"What do you mean too ugly?" Jasmine cried. "She's the most adorable horse I ever saw in my life!"

Roce burst into laughter. Wymon joined him. "He's just teasing you, Jasmine. I told you there are sides to my brothers you don't want to know about."

"I get it. How much do I owe you for this visit, Dr. Clayton?"

"That depends on how angry Wymon will be if I take money from you."

She held her stance. "This isn't about Wymon. You dropped everything at your practice to drive over here. If you won't tell me now, then I'll just send you a check."

"I'm afraid my big brother will go through the roof if I cash it."

"Is he that horrible?"

"You really don't want to know."

"Well, he doesn't know how horrible I can be if I don't get my own way. I'm an only child and am known for being impossible. Ask my parents and they'll tell you. I'm the little girl with the curl in the middle of her forehead. Never mind when she's good. But when she's bad…"

Laughter was still rippling out of both men when Jim rejoined them.

"Mr. Whitefeather? I would like to buy this filly. Shall we go to your office to do business?"

There was a gleam in Jim's eye. "Right this way."

Wymon watched her walk out of the barn with Jim without turning around.

Roce let out a whistle. "Well, what do you know?"

"I know it's time for you to get back to your office. Thanks for coming."

"I'm going. Let me know how soon there's going to be a wedding, so I can block some time away from work."

He shook his head. "You're full of it."

"Good grief. First Eli, now you. I'm starting to get nervous that it's contagious."

"It's not like that, Roce."

"Give me a break. It's exactly like that! You think I don't know my own brother? Just don't be surprised if Farnsworth comes around with a shotgun to blow up the wedding.

"I can't decide who's more gorgeous—the brown-and-white filly or the one with eyes as green as a lush meadow. I'm convinced you came upon that plane crash for a reason." He closed his doctor bag. "I'll be keeping close tabs on you."

After Roce walked out of the barn, Wymon remained in the stall, rubbing the filly's forelock.

*Wouldn't it be something if what Roce had said was true.*

"You're a lucky little horse to have a new owner like her, you know that?"

It didn't take long before Jasmine came back with Jim. He led the filly to the corral. They followed and said goodbye. Wymon had trouble tearing Jasmine away.

The filly stood at the fence and let out a long neigh as they walked off. Already the two had bonded. On the way to their cars he asked Jasmine what she planned to do.

"I think I'll bring the horse trailer tomorrow and take her home."

"I have a better idea. Why don't I meet you at your house in the morning, and I'll pull your trailer with my truck?"

"Only if you'll let me pay your brother." Her answer was all he could have hoped for. "Since he's younger than you, he has a medical practice to grow and needs all the income he can bring in."

"You're right. I promise I won't interfere. What time do you want to leave your house? I'll meet you there, and we'll drive to Missoula together."

"Mr. Whitefeather said I could come any time after ten tomorrow morning."

"Then I'll be at your house at nine."

She stared up at him. "How do I thank you? Your friend is wonderful, and I'm so happy to own a horse like this with such a fabulous pedigree."

"Have you decided on a name?"

"Not yet."

"Let's talk about it on the phone while we're driving. Give me your cell, and I'll put my number in."

"That'll be fun. Let me have yours, and I'll do the same."

Once they'd made the exchange, he helped her get in her car. "Drive safely."

"You, too."

It was getting harder and harder to leave her for any reason. Once they drove away, she phoned him. "How come you're still behind my car?"

"I'm making sure you get home safely."

"No, Wymon. Please, don't do that. It's too much driving."

"I like it."

"I'm getting more and more in your debt."

"I like that, too. What kind of a name do you have in mind?"

"I can think of dozens of names, but since seeing her, I think I want an Indian name in keeping with her heritage."

"Did Jim suggest any? He'd be the one to know."

"He mentioned five I couldn't pronounce."

"I'm sure you'll figure out the perfect name."

"Your horse has a great name. Titus sounds regal. I think it's a good Biblical name, too."

A smile broke out on Wymon's face. "Part of my English heritage. How about Marble?"

"Wymon—that's not Indian-sounding."

"If she were a he, you could call her Chief for Chief Joseph."

Now she was chuckling. "Be serious."

"I'm trying. How about Percette? The feminine of Nez Perce."

"Will you stop?"

"All right. I'll only suggest one more. What do you think of Moondrop?"

After a silence, "That's beautiful."

"I think so, too, but it's not Indian. She has polka dots that look like white moons dropped in milk chocolate. If my new little niece were to see your horse, she'd point to them and say the word 'moon' over and over again."

Jasmine chuckled. "That name is brilliant!"

"I'm glad you like it."

"That's what I'm going to call her."

"Maybe you should sleep on it before you make a decision. Once you call her that, you can't go back to anything else. Horses remember their names."

"I know. They have fantastic memories. Oh, this has been the most wonderful day!"

"It's not over yet. When we reach your house, how would you like to go to a movie? We'll grab some takeout on the way."

"I'd love it, but are you sure? You still have to drive back to Stevensville."

"Let me worry about that."

"You're spoiling me."

"I haven't had fun for a long time. Humor me. Now I'm afraid I have to hang up because I need to get off and fill the gas tank. I'll see you at your house in a few minutes."

"All right."

Jasmine hung up and headed for the turnoff leading to her parents' home. It had been such a perfect day—she was higher than a kite, as her father always said when he was happy.

But her spirits plunged when she saw Rob's familiar Escalade in the driveway. She had no idea how long he'd been there. He'd driven from Helena and had barged in on her parents. That meant Buzz had already run to him with the news that he'd seen her with Wymon in Drummond on the Fourth.

Her anger flared. How dare he come to her house after their phone call a few days ago! She pulled in next to his car. But before going inside, she phoned Wymon to tell him not to come. *Please, pick up.*

To Jasmin's chagrin, her call to Wymon came too late. He pulled in right behind her and got out of his truck just as Rob opened the front door and came walking toward them. His head bandage was gone. A clear Band-Aid had been put over the stitches. You would never have known he'd suffered a head injury.

Her heart plummeted as Rob's unfriendly gaze focused on Wymon. "Mr. Clayton? I guess I'm not surprised to see you here after learning you and Jasmine were together at the rodeo on the Fourth."

She was thankful Wymon didn't try to shake Rob's hand. "It's nice to see you up and walking, Mr. Farnsworth," Wymon said. "When I learned that Jasmine's horse had died, I told her about Jim Whitefeather, who breeds them. We've just come from picking one out for her."

Rob shot her a piercing glance. "I didn't think you were ready to buy a new one yet. You haven't even talked to me about it."

The blood pounded in her ears. "I didn't know how I felt until I saw this adorable Appaloosan."

"That's because we haven't been together since the hospital."

"If you two will excuse me, I have to get back to the ranch. Like I said, I'm happy to see that you're doing so well, Mr. Farnsworth." Wymon tipped his hat to both of them and climbed in the cab of his truck. Within seconds the rancher drove away, taking her heart with him.

She turned to Rob who was dressed in an expensive navy suit and tie. Her last conversation on the phone with him days ago hadn't made a dent. He'd come today prepared to take her out to eat. After talking to Buzz he was all fired up, but she couldn't allow this to go on and decided it was good Rob knew she'd gone to the rodeo with Wymon. It was time to have it out with him, but it was going to be painful.

Rob moved closer to her with a grim expression. "I know you didn't expect to see me today, but it appears you forgot about your promise to come to the rally with me on the sixteenth."

*What?* She'd thought he was going to light into her about the night of the fourth. "You don't expect me to attend that now, surely."

"Of course I do. My folks don't know about our argument on the phone. I'm planning on you being there."

She shook her head. "We didn't have an argument. I turned down your marriage proposal. That changes everything."

"I still can't believe you meant it, and I need you to be at the rally. You promised me. I can't disappoint my folks before then."

His intimidation tactics weren't going to work. "I'm sorry, Rob. You need to tell them the truth right away. They think things about us that aren't true."

"You're the coldest woman I ever met."

"Please, don't label me because you don't want to hear the truth. Ever since we started dating, you've had this fantasy about us, but it's one that has been in your mind, not mine. I heard it when you were talking about your new plane and all the things a family could fit into it.

"I've never seen us as a family, but I don't want to say things to hurt you. You have to know how proud I am of your accomplishments. You're going to go all the way in politics, I know it, and I want only the best for you, believe me. But you need a soul mate who can support your ambition and plan a life with you that makes you both whole!"

His lips thinned. "So I don't make you feel whole?" He simply couldn't hear what she was trying to tell him. "Isn't it interesting that your parents told me you'd gone to look at some horses for sale today, so I waited. I just didn't realize the big gun from the Sapphire ranch had been the one to put the thought in your head.

"The man moves fast when he sees something he wants. First he takes you to the Fourth of July celebration in Drummond. Now the trip today. How long have you known him? One week?" he lashed out.

"Not nearly as long as you have. I only met him the morning he saved us after the crash."

"How many times have you been with him since then that I don't know about?"

*Don't do this to yourself, Rob.* He would be shocked if he knew she'd taken him a gift the day she'd been released from the hospital. "You shouldn't have come here. There's nothing more to say. I made that clear on the phone."

With his brown hair and brown eyes, he was a good-looking man, but right now lines marred his features. "We haven't been together since the crash. How can you make such a serious judgment about us? We've been so good together."

"I agree we've had some great times, but there's all the difference in the world when you talk about getting married. I can't say yes to you because I don't feel it, and time won't alter that decision."

"Clayton is the reason you've changed so fast."

"How can you say that? I didn't know him from

Adam when we had our plane accident. He has nothing to do with my feelings for you. The more you and I saw each other, the more I realized we're not compatible. You *know* we're not.

"In the plane you accused me of resenting what you did for your career. That's just one example that you *did* sense we had problems, but didn't want to admit it. I don't resent what you do for a living, Rob, but I haven't been able to see myself fitting in to your lifestyle. That's why I've never gone flying with you. I didn't want to encourage you that way. Don't you see? It just wouldn't work."

He took a quick breath. "Then at least do me this one favor. Come to the rally with me next Saturday in Helena. It'll be in the exhibit hall at the Lewis and Clark Fairgrounds. After it's over, I swear I'll tell my folks the truth. But I can't disappoint them on this."

Rob's life was tied up with his parents. Their bond ran his life to a great extent. He needed to be his own man, but being their only child made that difficult. She could see that, and she felt sorry for him, but she had to be strong right now.

"I couldn't, Rob. It would be dishonest."

"Why?"

"Because we'll never be a couple."

He winced. "Would it kill you to pretend for one more week? The rally is a high point for me. There'll be others until November, but not in Helena. After it's over, there's a long time before the vote. By then my parents will have accepted that we're not together anymore and there won't be any expectations. Can you do that much for me?"

She knew how much this rally meant to him. He lived for nights like that. So did his parents. Jasmine also remembered that his expertise as a pilot had saved their lives. She did owe him for that and decided she could do him this last favor, though she knew it was against her better judgment.

"If I do it, I won't go up on the platform with you. I'll sit down in front with everyone else where your parents can see me. That's as much as I'd be prepared to do."

"Thank you for that, Jasmine," he said in a quiet voice. "I'll call you next Saturday morning to let you know when I'm picking you up."

"No, Rob. I'll come to the fairgrounds alone. If you can't live with that, then I won't come at all."

After a long pause he said, "The rally starts at six, but you'll need to be there by five. Security will watch for you and make sure you get a place right up in front."

"All right. I'm going inside now."

While they'd been talking, her thoughts hadn't strayed from Wymon who'd handled this encounter with the kind of diplomacy that was his trademark. Wymon was the grown-up. Though they'd had plans to go to a show, he hadn't pushed it. She knew he wouldn't be back today.

As Wymon had told her earlier, Rob wasn't the kind of man to take no for an answer, and he was giving her space to deal with it. Everything Wymon did made him an exceptional man. Already her feelings for him were off the charts.

Rob's blistering gaze hurt. "So this is how it ends," he said.

This was a nightmare. "What do you want me to do?"

"When did you learn to be so cruel? I wish I'd never laid eyes on you."

No one in the world liked losing, but Rob had a particularly hard time because of his competitive spirit. He got in his car. After he backed out, his tires screeched as he took off down the street in the opposite direction from Wymon. By now the rancher was miles away. She'd have to call him in a few minutes.

Her parents met her at the front door. "I'm sorry you had to deal with him," she said. "Buzz must have called him and told him he'd seen me at the rodeo with Wymon on the Fourth. I realize now how much that must have hurt. Especially when Rob never told Buzz that Wymon was the person who rescued us."

"His pride prevented him from saying anything," her father murmured.

"Days ago, Rob called me, and I had to tell him it was over between us. But he's in denial and I don't know how long it's going to last. He came over here today to remind me of my promise to go to his rally next Saturday in Helena."

"Oh dear," her mom said.

"Oh dear is right. I know how much he was counting on it, so I told him I'd go for one last time. But I said I'd get there by myself and sit with the audience. It's as much as I can do. I'm just sorry you had to deal with him. I know he likes you two a lot and hoped you'd be able to influence me."

Her father shook his head. "He'll get over his disappointment in time."

"I hope so. I'm just thankful he's fully recovered from the crash. I'm very much aware of how difficult this is for him. I feel so sorry it had to end this way, but he has to know we aren't meant to be together."

"When it's not right, it's not right, honey." Her mom put an arm around her shoulders, and they walked inside the house.

Yet how incredible was it that if Jasmine hadn't agreed to go with him for that flight, she would never have met Wymon Clayton? Since meeting him, she couldn't imagine life without him.

"Well?" her father asked once they were in the living room. "What's the word on the horse?"

"I bought the sweetest filly from Mr. Whitefeather today. Wymon is going to come by tomorrow and help me bring her home from Missoula. When you see her coat, you'll know why I've named her Moondrop."

Her mom smiled. "That's a beautiful name."

"It was Wymon's idea," she said, blushing. And thought what a fool in love she was.

After excusing herself, she hurried to her room to call Wymon. To her disappointment her call went to his voice mail. He was probably on the phone doing ranch business with his brother Eli.

She left the message for him to call her back so she could tell him what had happened with Rob.

# *Chapter Six*

By six in the morning Wymon had gone up to the north pasture to inspect the fencing. He'd always heard his mother complain under her breath that the housework was never done. It was the same for the fencing. You couldn't go a day without noticing a portion of the miles of fencing had been knocked down somewhere. Sure enough, the cattle would find it, then they'd all have to spend a day bringing them back.

This morning he didn't mind. He needed work to help the time pass faster until he left for Philipsburg. Jasmine's phone call to explain what had happened with Farnsworth yesterday didn't surprise him. Wymon had an adversary in the man who reminded him of his bull-riding days.

When he glanced up, he noticed that the sky had darkened with clouds over the Sapphires. A summer storm was building. He knew the signs, but it was still three, maybe four hours away.

"Good grief! You beat me up here!"

Wymon looked over his shoulder at Eli. Some of

the stockmen were still jumping out of the truck. Others were on horseback. "Yup. I thought I'd better put in my time early this morning."

Eli walked over to his side. "Yeah? Got plans later?"

*Here it comes.* Eli's happy marriage had opened him up like nothing else. "As a matter of fact, I do."

"Roce says Ms. Telford is one beautiful woman."

His brother would be right about that. The family telegraph was in perfect running order. "Then I guess he told you Jim Whitefeather sold her the filly. I'm going to go with her to pick her up."

"He says the Appaloosan is almost as pretty as she is."

"That sounds like Roce."

"I heard the pilot you saved was Representative Farnsworth, the one fighting your grizzly reintroduction program."

"Yup."

"Did he know who you were?"

Wymon turned to him and tipped his hat back. "We recognized each other. Both he and his parents phoned to thank me for dragging him out of the cockpit. I appreciated his call."

But any civility between them disappeared yesterday when Farnsworth saw him drive up to Jasmine's house and he put two and two together that things were already serious between them.

One of Eli's brows lifted when he was worried. "Does he know you're taking out his girlfriend?"

*Hell.* If anyone else had asked him that question...

"Afraid so. His manager saw me with Jasmine at the Drummond rodeo on the Fourth. Even though she's told Rob goodbye, he showed up at her house yesterday as I was pulling in behind her, obviously hoping for a showdown. If his eyes had been weapons... He now knows for sure she's not his girlfriend anymore."

"Whoa."

"Whoa is right. I have a gut feeling Farnsworth isn't about to give up. I'm afraid the situation is getting uglier." It made Wymon anxious to see her again today.

Eli's features relaxed into a smile. "Whatever went on with them before the plane crash, she's been with you ever since. If she'd met you first, there'd be no Rob in her life. So you're doing something right, bro." He slapped him on the shoulder.

Only time would tell... A change of subject was in order. "How are your two favorite cowgirls?"

"I swear life couldn't get any better."

With Eli so in love, the change in mood around the Clayton ranch was nothing sort of miraculous. "I'm happy for you, Eli."

"That works both ways." His eyes lit up. "Have fun with the fillies, if you know what I mean. Now I'd better get going before the downpour starts. Luis is waiting for me. It's past time we started moving the cattle to the other pasture. This one is close to getting overgrazed."

Wymon chuckled as Eli hurried to join the crew. *Have fun with the fillies.* Good advice. That was exactly what he intended to do.

An hour later he got back in his truck and drove down the mountain to shower and change into a long-sleeved plaid shirt. After eating a mixing bowl full of cereal with a quart of milk, he took off with a feeling of excitement he hadn't experienced in years. No, that wasn't true. Wymon had never felt like this before.

He was still breathless remembering dancing with her and the way her body felt when he pulled her close. He'd never forget that moment in the truck when he'd leaned across to cup her face. The desire to kiss her had come close to overwhelming him. Today he knew for a fact that if they got that close again, it was going to happen.

By the time he reached Philipsburg, the wind had started to kick up. He'd been listening to the radio. This whole part of the state had received storm warnings. He called Jasmine to tell her he was almost at her parents' house.

"I'm glad you made it before the storm."

"It won't hit for another hour."

"I hope not. Just pull around to the barn. My horse trailer is next to it. I'll meet you there."

His heart leaped when he saw her standing by her truck. She was a gorgeous sight in a white cowboy hat and boots. He loved her white, long-sleeved Western shirt with its snap fasteners. The belt with the big buckle drew his gaze to her womanly figure. Over her arm hung a deerskin leather jacket with fringe. The woman had great style.

"Good morning," he called out the window and backed up the truck to the horse trailer. "Why don't you get in the cab out of the wind while I fasten the hitch?"

"It's kind of tricky."

"If I can't figure it out, I'll call for help."

Her smile lit up his universe. "You're the first man I've ever met who admitted to the possibility."

"Is that good or bad?" He climbed out from the driver's seat.

"Don't you know?" The twinkle in her green eyes kept his heart thudding.

After several attempts, he finally hooked it up and climbed back in the truck. He slanted her a glance. "For a minute there, I was afraid I'd have to ask for your help."

"You want to know a secret? The first time Dad tried to fasten it to the hitch on my truck, it took him half an hour. Wait till I tell him!"

"Maybe you shouldn't. According to my mother, men's egos are fragile."

"You're right. On second thought I'll tell my *mom* instead."

He broke into laughter before starting the engine. Wymon never knew what was going to come out of her mouth next. She had the power to entertain him indefinitely.

On the way out of town she looked over at him. "I'm sorry about yesterday. I had no idea Rob would be at my house."

"Don't worry about it."

"He had no right to come all the way to Philipsburg and he was in a terrible mood. I'm so glad you

left when you did. I've never seen him upset like that
before. Between the crash and my rejection, he's in
a lot of pain and that hurts me."

"I'm sorry. If I were he, I wouldn't be able to give
up so fast on you either, believe me."

"Yes you would, because you understand the word
'no,'" she said quietly. "You're a different kind of
man."

Wymon took a deep breath. "What kind is that?"

"Someone who knows how to handle difficult situ-
ations and make the right decisions. When you came
on the accident scene, you knew exactly what to do
and how. Your quiet calm helped me more than you
can imagine."

"Did it ever occur to you I was terrified?"

She laughed as if what he'd said was absurd,
pleasing him to no end.

The closer they got to Missoula, he saw flashes of
lightning, and the wind grew stronger. It started to
buffet the truck and trailer. "I can tell you one thing.
If we start to load Moondrop when the storm hits,
she'll get spooked. I'm going to call Jim and tell him
we're going to be late."

"That's a good idea. The last thing I want is for my
new little baby to have a bad experience while I'm
trying to take her home. She'll remember it."

Jasmine had a horse whisperer's instincts combined with an innate sweetness that tugged at his
heart. "We can't have that. What do you say we stop
for breakfast until the worst of it passes over?"

"That sounds wonderful. I was too excited to eat this morning."

"I know a place on the outskirts where Roce and I often meet when he can't be away from the hospital too long. Then we'll head out to Jim's ranch."

After he'd phoned Jim, he turned off the freeway and headed for the diner he had in mind. Tumbleweeds and small bits of debris were rolling across the road before he pulled into the parking lot. She looked at the sign. "The Velvet Couch? What a strange name!"

He turned off the engine, angling his head toward her. "You never heard that term?" She shook her head. "It's cowboy lingo for 'bedroll.' You know the old chuck-line riders who'd show up on the range? They'd set out their bedrolls around the campfire for the night, hoping for a little chow."

Her mouth curved into a big smile. "A *couch*! I learn something new every time I'm with you."

"Stick with me, babe. Come on. I've got to hustle you inside. We're about to get baptized." He jumped down from the cab and walked around. When he opened her door, another gust of wind with the taste of rain hit them both in the face. "Hold on to your hat." He put his arm around her waist, and they hurried inside just as the hail started.

The diner was only half-full. Old black-and-white photos of Montana in the late 1890s covered the walls. He guided them to a booth with a menu holder farther away from the others and slid in next to her so he could feel her warmth. They both removed their hats. He brushed them off and put them on the other side of the table.

A familiar face approached. "Hey, Wymon."

"Jake!"

He poured the steaming brew into their cups. "You didn't duck in here a moment too soon. Will you listen to that clatter? Where's the doc?"

"At work, I hope. Meet a friend of mine. Jasmine Telford, this is Jake Simonds, the manager of the Velvet Couch."

"How do you do, Jake? Wymon was just telling me the meaning of the name."

The older man grinned. "Some people think it's a house of ill repute. That's okay if it brings in customers. I'll fix you the breakfast special. Hen-fruit stir with long sweetenin', cackleberries and overland trout."

The look on her face made both men chuckle.

Wymon nodded. "Make that two orders and keep the coffee coming."

Country music might have been playing from the jukebox, but the rage of the storm pretty well drowned out every sound. First lightning flashed, then thunder cannonaded across the sky over and over. They felt the rumble beneath their feet.

While she reacted to the violence, the lights went out. "Oh, no," everyone murmured at the same time.

Wymon put his arm around her shoulders and gave her a hug. "This is better than lying around a camp fire on our couch getting soaking wet," he said into her fragrant hair. To his disappointment the lights went back on. When her body shook with silent laughter, he removed his arm, but it took all his strength of will not to kiss her into next week first.

"Here we are." Jake had arrived with their food. "Two plates of bacon, eggs and pancakes with our own huckleberry syrup!"

"I might have known," she cried softly. The older man chuckled. "It appears the loss of electricity didn't bother you."

"We have our own power source, ma'am."

"Of course. I must say this looks delicious."

"We aim to please."

After he left, they dug into their food. While she ate, she studied the menu. "I take it the eggs are the cackleberries, but I don't know why."

Wymon nodded, relishing his food as if he hadn't already eaten earlier. "It's an old English expression from the 1880s. A hen cackled when it laid an egg."

"So the egg is the berry?"

He nodded with a smile.

"Probably your great-grandfathers used the expression when they came over from Lancashire."

She remembered! "Probably," he said with a grin.

"And the sweetenin'?"

"Old-fashioned molasses. My ancestors enjoyed it as a sweetener they called treacle. It was thought to have healthful benefits."

"It's another language."

"On our cattle roundups, Luis, the foreman, is known to read aloud from a book on cowboy jargon to entertain the crew. They love it."

Her eyes widened. "I can see my education is lacking. If there's a book, I'm going to buy it."

"There are dozens of them."

"That would be a fun thing to give my parents for Christmas."

The storm continued to do its worst while Wymon chatted away with the most fascinating woman this side of the Continental Divide.

Jake came out a few minutes later. "Can I get you anything else?"

"Do you still have that Edgar Potter book on cowboy slang?"

"Yup. It's on the shelf in my office."

"Would you be kind enough to let Jasmine take a look at it?"

"It would be my pleasure." He was back within a minute.

Wymon took it from him and handed it to Jasmine. "This author was born in 1895 in North Dakota and wrote three books on the Old West."

She reached eagerly for it and read aloud some of the alphabetized terms in the middle.

*Railroad Bible: a deck of cards; Randy: wanton, lecherous; Ranny: top cowhand; Rappee: inferior snuff; Rattler: freight train; Rattle your Hocks: hurry up.*

"I can't believe all these funny words. My dad has got to read this book!" Jasmine turned to him with a flush on her lovely face. "I'm so glad you brought me here!"

*So am I.*

Together they looked through it and chuckled. Pretty soon he saw other people leaving. "Jasmine? The storm has passed over. If I can tear you away from this long enough, we'll go get Moondrop. I'll pay the bill and give it back to Jake."

"Tell him thank you for letting me see the book and for the delicious meal. The Couch's version of sweetenin' was awesome."

"May I quote you?"

"Definitely."

They left for Jim's ranch. Wymon loved the smell of the earth after a cloudburst like this. Everything felt fresh and alive. He felt alive like never before. A half hour later he helped load Moondrop into the one-stall trailer.

"She loads so nicely, Wymon. I just can't believe how wonderful she is! It's going to be a joy to train her."

"Jim's the best at what he does."

"I can see that." Jasmine had brought a net of green grass hay. "Once we reach the barn at home, I'll set out her necessary feed. Oh, you little darling." She kissed her nose and forelock. "I'd like to ride back here with you, but I can't. Wymon will drive slowly so you don't panic. Okay? Here's a Fancy Filly treat."

Wymon watched her pull one out of her pocket and feed it to her horse. Curious he asked, "What kind is it?"

"A peppermint patty. Would you believe it's *molasses* based with oatmeal and flaxseed?" Her smiling gaze met his. "More of that wonderful sweetenin'."

If she looked at him again like that, they weren't going anywhere for a long time.

The filly chomped away and nudged Jasmine to get more of them. She giggled like a young girl. "So... you liked that, huh?"

Wymon made certain Moondrop was tied securely, and then signaled it was time to go. But tearing Jasmine away from her new baby wasn't an easy task. "The sooner we get her home, the sooner you can play with her."

After he shut the door, Jim saw them off. "Thank you for everything," Jasmine called to him from her open window. "I'm so thrilled."

"She's found a fine home with you. So long, Wymon. Talk to you later in the week!"

"I'll call you, Jim. Thank you!"

As Wymon drove away, he wished he was driving them straight to the Clayton ranch. After putting the new filly to bed, he'd like to take Jasmine to his loft where they could watch the sun go down over the Sapphire Mountains. He'd never ached for anything so much in his whole life.

No longer did he marvel over how fast Eli had fallen for Brianna and how he'd wanted to be married as soon as possible. Wymon had only known Jasmine a short time, yet already he recognized what was happening to him.

"What horse have you been riding since you lost Trixie?"

Jasmine shot Wymon a sideward glance. "I ride my mother's mare when she's not home."

One eyebrow lifted. "Now you have one of your own again."

"Moondrop is gorgeous. I'm so happy. Thank you so much for everything, Wymon." The light in her green eyes said it all. "My parents are home today. They've wanted to thank you in person for what you did and are looking forward to meeting you."

"I feel the same way. They've raised a wonderful daughter."

Color seeped into her high cheekbones. "I'm not wonderful."

"I saw the courageous thing you did at the crash site. Today I watched the way you wooed Moondrop until she was eating out of your hand. Those qualities tell me a lot about Jasmine Telford and her family."

She was looking out the window. "If you want to know the truth, I've done a lot of things I'm not proud of."

"We all make mistakes. Want to tell me what's troubling you on this exciting day?"

"You notice everything," she murmured.

"Forget I asked that question. It's none of my business."

Her head whipped around so she could look at him. "It's more your business than you realize."

"If I don't miss my guess, this is about Mr. Farnsworth."

"Yes. It's going to take me time to forget my conversation with Rob yesterday. Frankly, it was a confrontation. Thank heaven you were spared some of it."

Wymon sucked in his breath. "He hasn't liked my

politics for a long time, so meeting him face-to-face hasn't helped."

"It's not just you he reacted to. He was too intent on telling me how cruel I was. I'm afraid if you or anyone else had pulled in the driveway just then, he would have ripped your head off. He was in that kind of a mood, but I know it was because he was hurting."

A troubled sigh escaped her lips. "The timing of our breakup with the crash created the perfect storm. That's what has made me feel so guilty."

He blinked. "What are you saying exactly?"

"I didn't want to go on our last date because I realized my feelings weren't there for him. But I followed through because I thought I'd give myself one more chance to examine my reservations. To my shock he'd planned for us to fly to Seattle in his new plane. It was the last thing I wanted to do, but we were already at the airfield before I realized what he'd been planning."

"Had you flown with him before?"

"No. Never. I told him I didn't feel right about it because he flew for his job, and I didn't want to interfere with that. He accused me of resenting his career. I told him that wasn't true. To prove it, I told him I'd fly with him this one time."

Farnsworth knew how to manipulate. That was one of his best political tools.

"Once we'd reached cruising speed over the mountains, he suddenly proposed to me. He did it right there! I'd known something big was going on in his mind, but not while we were in the air. Rob had put

# FREE Merchandise is 'in the Cards' for you!

Dear Reader,

### *We're giving away FREE MERCHANDISE!*

Seriously, we'd like to reward you for reading this novel by giving you **FREE MERCHANDISE** worth over $20 retail. And no purchase is necessary!

You see the Jack of Hearts sticker above? Paste that sticker in the box on the Free Merchandise Voucher inside. Return the Voucher today… and we'll send you Free Merchandise!

Thanks again for reading one of our novels—and enjoy your Free Merchandise with our compliments!

*Pam Powers*

Pam Powers

P.S. Look inside to see what Free Merchandise is **"in the cards"** for you!

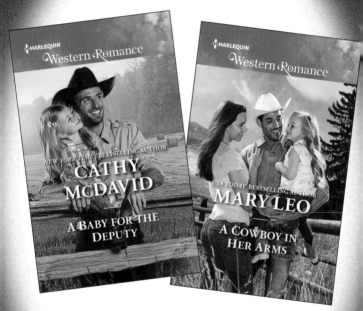

# YOUR FREE MERCHANDISE INCLUDES...
2 FREE Books **AND** 2 FREE Mystery Gifts

## FREE MERCHANDISE VOUCHER

2 FREE
BOOKS
and
2 FREE
GIFTS

Please send my Free Merchandise, consisting of
**2 Free Books** and **2 Free Mystery Gifts**.
I understand that I am under no obligation to buy
anything, as explained on the back of this card.

### 154/354 HDL GLTC

*Please Print*

FIRST NAME

LAST NAME

ADDRESS

APT.#          CITY

STATE/PROV.    ZIP/POSTAL CODE

## NO PURCHASE NECESSARY!

WR-517-FM17

me on the spot, and I had to answer him honestly, that I wasn't in love the way you have to be to contemplate marriage."

"Good grief. The perfect storm is right."

"Exactly. And while he was reacting to that, the hawk hit the propeller and the windshield shattered. He couldn't have avoided it, of course. I know that. And because he's such an outstanding pilot, he landed us safely despite his pain. I feel so awful about not being able to love him and make things right. That's what has been troubling me."

He reached for her hand. "You've both been through a harrowing ordeal. It's no wonder you're still trying to deal with it. Even if you've told him goodbye, he obviously needs more time until it all sinks in. You need more space, too, so after I drop you off at your ranch, I'm going to give it to you, Jasmine."

"No," she cried with tears in her eyes and clung to his hand. "That's the last thing I want. I only told you this because you were first at the scene and saw Rob at my house after I told you it was over. I wanted to be honest with you, Wymon. Please, don't let what I've told you change things between us."

Her urgency, plus the acknowledgement of the *us* between them, did what nothing else could have done.

"I won't."

After squeezing her hand, he let it go so he could concentrate on his driving. Wymon was transporting precious cargo. He decided they needed to change the subject so he turned on the radio to a country music station. They listened to tunes the rest of the way to Philipsburg.

Her parents walked out to the trailer while they were unloading Moondrop. "Well, will you look at that?" her father said with a big smile. Jasmine's blonde mother hurried over to the filly, running a hand over her neck and back, acting as familiar as her daughter with the horse.

"She's absolutely a beauty, honey."

Jasmine was beaming. "I think so, too. Mom? Dad? Meet Wymon Clayton from the Clayton Ranch."

Her dad shook Wymon's hand hard. "How can we ever thank you for helping our daughter? Talking to you on the phone wasn't enough to convey our gratitude."

"I just happened on them at the right moment."

"It was more than that. Jasmine has told us all about it." Her mother gave him a hug. He could see where Jasmine's good looks came from.

"Wymon?" Jasmine smiled at him. "I'm going to give her some water and take her to the corral so she'll get used to her surroundings."

Her father nodded. "Good idea. Our horses are there, too. They'll be friends in no time."

Together the three of them followed Jasmine around to the other side. The mare and the gelding perked up their heads and started walking toward Jasmine who led Moondrop inside. She talked to her horse as if she was a person, delighting Wymon who was still reacting to what they'd talked about in the truck.

*Please, don't let what I've told you change things between us.* She'd made it more than clear that she wanted to go on seeing him. That was all he'd needed to hear.

As she walked the Appaloosa around, the other horses trailed after her. He noticed her father put an arm around her mother's shoulders while they watched their daughter pass out treats and do her magic. She was like the beautiful Pied Piper of Philipsburg. Wymon was enchanted by the sight.

In a minute Mr. Telford walked over to Wymon who was undoing the hitch. "You figured out how to do that thing? I have trouble with it every time."

Wymon smiled to himself, recalling what Jasmine had told him. "It took me a while," he said.

"That makes me feel better." Both men grinned. "I wanted you to know that I applaud your efforts to get the grizzly reintroduced here. It's a damn shame the governor isn't onboard yet, but that doesn't have to be the end of it, right?"

"It's not," he said. "I'm working on some more funding measures as we speak."

"Good for you. I don't know if Jasmine has told you about the time we had the rare opportunity to see a mother grizzly and her two babies up at the Coffin Lakes when Jasmine was just a girl. She wanted to take one of the cubs back with us."

A chuckle broke out of Wymon, and that got her father started. "When she was young, she was always bringing home all kinds of critters she found, and that was in addition to our pet dog, rabbit, hamster, turtle and later a parrot. She loved anything she could mother. Thankfully, when she got her first pony, her obsession with all the other critters came to an end."

Wymon could relate. "With four rambunctious sons, my mother could swap similar stories with you and your wife. We were always bringing home snakes and other reptiles, much to my mother's chagrin. Speaking of my brothers, I don't know if Jasmine told you that my brother Roce checked out her horse yesterday. He's a vet in Missoula and gave Moondrop a clean bill of health."

"Jasmine was very pleased and impressed, especially with the care he took with her teeth. Did she tell you what happened to Trixie?"

"Not yet. I haven't wanted to ask her until she was ready to talk about it."

"Her horse died from a massive infection that spread so fast it couldn't be stopped in time. Jasmine noticed a bad-smelling discharge coming from her nose and jaw and felt guilty that she hadn't spotted it sooner. Pretty soon Trixie was tilting her head and stopped eating because one side of her jaw was much more swollen than the other. Our vet tried everything, but the infection was too severe."

"We've had animals die at the ranch. I know from personal experience it breaks your heart."

He nodded. "Her depression was so bad, I feared she couldn't bring herself to get another horse." His hazel eyes glistened as he looked at Wymon. "Besides helping save her life, you've been the one to get her back in the saddle again, so to speak. Her mother and I are more grateful than you know."

"Jim Whitefeather and I share a love of horses. This was pure fun for us."

"Hey, you two," Jasmine's mother called to them. "Come in the house and freshen up. We're having a picnic out on the patio. Jasmine? Leave Moondrop in the corral—she'll be fine!"

Wymon and Jasmine's father shared a smile.

"Coming!" Mr. Telford shouted, and the two men headed up to the house.

# Chapter Seven

Jasmine had seen her father's and Wymon's heads bent together in conversation while he'd been unhitching the trailer. She couldn't help but wonder what they were talking about, but she could tell it was friendly by the way they smiled. They seemed comfortable with each other, which was a relief for her as her father didn't always warm up to strangers right away.

Once they'd assembled on the patio for a late lunch, Wymon caught her eye. She felt he was sending her a special message, and she couldn't wait to be alone with him.

After a meal of mouth-watering fried chicken, potato salad and homemade ice cream, she asked Wymon to walk her back to the corral. Jasmine wanted to be alone with him before he left for the drive back to Stevensville.

She caught up to Moondrop and led her to the stall in the barn that had once been Trixie's. Until now she hadn't thought she could stand to see another horse in her place. But the old adage about time healing all wounds was true in this case. Still, she suffered from a surfeit of guilt about what had happened with Rob.

To her consternation, Wymon had picked up on it. While the two of them rubbed her horse down, he looked at her. "What's wrong, Jasmine? Are you still mourning Trixie? Your father told me what happened to her."

"I'm over that, and I'm glad Dad told you."

"Then you're still upset about Rob."

She was blown away by his instincts. "I've had enough time to figure things out. What I'm feeling is terrible guilt because I know I used Rob to help me get over my pain of losing my horse. He filled a need in me that led him to believe I cared for him more than I did. Now my guilt is weighing me down. It's the reason I didn't cut off our relationship sooner. Does that make any sense to you?"

Before she could guess his intentions, he reached for her and pulled her into his arms, rocking her gently. Feeling his hard body against hers sent shock waves through her nervous system.

"You didn't do it intentionally. You have to let it go," he whispered against her cheek. "People will be voting in November. You've filled a need for him, too. There's nothing wrong with both of you needing each other to get through tough times. It's life."

He made such wonderful sense it was screaming at her. "You're right. I'm so glad I met you."

"You took the words right out of my mouth."

His lips sought hers and coaxed them apart in a hungry kiss that took her breath away. At first contact, she lost cognizance of her surroundings while she reveled in the taste and feel of him. This was what she'd been craving for weeks.

He was all male and so desirable—it made her tremble to think such a man existed. This amazing rancher who'd appeared on the accident scene like a modern knight to the rescue was kissing her as if his life depended on it.

"You're so beautiful, Jasmine. Heaven help me, but I want you."

His hands ran up and down her back, arching her closer until there was no air between them.

*"Wymon—"* A moan of pleasure escaped her throat as she slid her arms around his neck, needing his kiss like she needed air.

"If you want me to stop, I don't think I can," he responded, his voice ragged. "You're going to have to help me."

"I can't, because I don't want this to end," she whispered before covering his rugged features with kiss after kiss. He chased her mouth and began devouring her.

The rapture he created wasn't like anything she'd experienced in her life. Her world spun with every touch, every caress. She almost went into shock when he suddenly tore his lips from hers and held her at arm's length with a groan.

"I want to take you away where we can be alone for weeks on end, but we can't do this, Jasmine. Not here. Not now. It's a good thing I'm going to be busy this week talking to ranchers and potential donors. I don't trust myself around you. Maybe after a week, I'll have gotten myself under control."

"You have a lot more control than I do." Embarrassed that her voice was shaking, she eased away from him and patted her filly's neck.

"If you don't have any plans for next Saturday, I'll drive here after my committee meeting with the governor in Helena and we'll spend the rest of the day together."

*Helena?*

"How does that sound?"

"I'd love it, but I do have a commitment I have to keep on Saturday."

"For your job at the university? I thought you were taking your vacation then."

Her heartbeat doubled. There was no way around this because she didn't want there to be any secrets between them. "I will be on summer break then, but I made a promise to Rob I have to keep." She told him what had transpired yesterday in her parents' driveway and that she planned to attend the rally in Helena.

Wymon stared at her in the semidarkness of the barn. She could hear him thinking. "I have an idea. If you could get a ride to Helena, I could pick you up after the rally and drive you back to Philipsburg," he said.

"You would do that?" The excitement in her voice thrilled him.

"What do you think? Though I love talking on the

phone with you while we're in separate cars, I much prefer you to sit right next to me."

Heat filled her cheeks. "I'm sure my parents would take me. In fact I know they would be happy that I wouldn't have to drive home alone at night."

"It would make *me* happy, too," he said. "So why don't we do this? I'll stay in Helena after the committee meeting is adjourned. Give me a call when the rally is over. I'll be in my dark blue Audi. We'll meet in the parking lot and find a restaurant to have dinner."

"I'd love that. The rally starts at six, and should come to an end by seven or seven-thirty at the latest."

"Perfect, then I'll drive you home and we'll put Moondrop to bed."

Heaven. "But I feel guilty making you wait in Helena so long for me."

"I'll have plenty to do while I'm there."

"Then I can't wait," she said.

"It's going to be a long week, but it'll be worth it. Come and walk me out to my truck." He rubbed Moondrop's forelock. "Be a good girl and mind Jasmine. See you soon." He grasped Jasmine's hand, and they left the barn.

When they reached the truck, he cupped her face in his hands and gave her a long, hard kiss that made her go weak with longing. "I'll phone you before Saturday. I want a daily progress report on Moondrop."

He'd said "daily," making her feel euphoric.

She couldn't bear it when he climbed in the cab and drove away from her. When she couldn't see his taillights any longer, she hurried back into the barn to say good-night to Moondrop. After closing the barn doors, she dashed to the rear entrance of the ranch house.

Her parents had gone to bed. She was glad because when she looked in the bathroom mirror, there was no question she'd been thoroughly kissed. Her parents would notice the rash caused by the rasp of his hard jaw. Those electrifying moments in his arms had transported her to a place she'd never been before. She could never get enough of him. It wasn't possible.

Sleep didn't come for a long time. She could still smell him and relived every single moment from the time he'd taken care of her at the crash scene to their parting tonight. There was no one in the world like him. If he didn't feel the same way about her, then she was headed for a heartache she didn't want to think about.

Between training Moondrop and finishing up some work at the university, she'd stay busy until next Saturday when she could be with him again. She knew her parents wouldn't mind driving her to Helena, not when they heard Wymon would be bringing her home.

What if she'd never met him? It made her stomach sick to think about it.

*I'm so in love with him, I'll never be the same again.*

EARLY WEDNESDAY MORNING on his way to join the stockmen in the upper pasture, Wymon drove to the Clayton Sapphire Gem Shop farther up the mountain road. His family owned a mine that had supplied sapphires for years from the very mountains he loved.

His father had built the gem shop for his mother to run. What had started out as a hobby had turned into a career for her. Over the years she'd made a name for herself in the sapphire business and continued to receive orders from all over the country.

Today he was on a special mission for one and hoped to get to the shop before she arrived at nine. He checked his watch. Six thirty. That was good. He didn't want her to know what he'd been up to.

After parking in front, he let himself in with the key and walked through to the back room where he opened the safe. His mother kept her most prized sapphires locked up inside. When much younger, he and his brothers had spent plenty of hours up there with her, poring over her inventory for amusement. The sapphires came in a wide assortment of hues, and each brother had his favorites.

Wymon remembered one sapphire that was an unusual spring-green color. He hadn't thought about it in years until he'd looked into Jasmine's eyes at the crash site. They were identical in color to the stone. He wondered if his mother had sold it a long time ago, or if it was still in the safe.

She kept the different colored stones separated in little velvet bags. Using his flashlight, he started looking in each bag of gems, reminding him of happy times in his youth. The last bag had to contain the green ones.

He reached for a square of velvet on a worktable

and poured them out to get a good look. The greens came in different shades. As he separated them, the spring-green stone seemed to wink up at him.

His mother hadn't sold it!

Excited, he put it in his hand and focused the flashlight on it. The round solitaire had to be at least two carats and had a hidden green fire like Jasmine's eyes. Without hesitation, he found an empty velvet bag and put the stone inside it.

Once he'd slipped it in his pocket, he put the other stones back in the bag and stored everything away in the safe. Like a thief in the night, he quietly left the shop and headed up to the pasture with his precious quarry. He had plans for it. Later he'd tell his mother what he'd done and pay her full price.

When Saturday arrived three days later, he left early for Helena and stopped at a jewelry store on his way to the state capitol building.

"May I help you, sir?"

"Yes. I have a green sapphire here I'd like mounted on a wide gold band."

The man took a look at it through his loupe. "This is an extraordinary stone with an exceptional cut and vivid saturation. I don't think I've ever seen one quite like it."

"It came from my family's mine in the Sapphires."

He stared at Wymon. "You're talking the Clayton mine? Your mother runs the shop?"

"That's right."

"She's an excellent jeweler herself."

"She is, but I don't want her to know about this."

The other man nodded. "Give me a minute, and I'll show you what I have."

Within ten minutes Wymon had picked the band he wanted plus a thin wedding band to match. "Can you have everything ready by later this afternoon? I'll only be in Helena today."

"I'll put a rush on it."

"Thank you. I'll be back."

With little time to spare, he drove to the state capitol where Jim was waiting for him. Together they joined the committee of ranchers and sat around the conference room table where the governor presided with his circle of advisers.

Their eleven o'clock meeting ran through the lunch hour until two thirty. They presented all their latest findings and had legal representation there to answer any questions from the men who worked closest with the governor.

Wymon's adrenaline was working overtime because they'd be hearing the governor's decision any minute now. Jim's brow was furrowed. He darted Wymon a glance he read perfectly. They were going to lose this round again.

Yup. They'd wanted the governor's backing.

The most outspoken of their adversaries—chief among them Rob Farnsworth—had done their homework over the last six months and were using scare tactics to combat their plan. No matter how accurately Wymon's side had presented the facts—that the Yellowstone grizzly population was accepted by the public, that there'd only been eight fatal attacks by bears in 140 years, that grizzly bears didn't go after livestock—their ears were closed.

The governor cleared his throat. "Gentlemen? You ranchers and wild life experts who want the grizzlies introduced back into the Sapphires have presented a strong and passionate argument on this issue.

"We appreciate the statistics you've accumulated and your reasoning. But I'm afraid the consensus for now is to wait until next January when the legislature is in session. That will be the best time to propose a new bill. The public still needs more educating on this issue. I wish you well."

The governor's response came as no surprise. Dejected, but not devastated, Wymon shook the governor's hand and walked out of the room with the other committee members. They parted company on the steps of the capitol and agreed to meet in two weeks to brainstorm ideas and start working on preparing another bill.

Jim's gaze met Wymon's. "Let's get lunch."

"I'll follow you."

They headed to Tiny's Grill. Wymon pulled his Montana map out of the glove compartment and took it inside with him. Over steak sandwichs, they worked out a new battle plan, outlining the geographic areas they needed to focus on.

"We're going to have to do a thorough canvassing, Wymon. Door-to-door visits, signatures, pledges, the works!"

"Agreed. That's why I turned down the job with

the Cattlemen's Association. I've freed myself up. Let's do it together."

"My wife will handle the horse sales while I'm gone."

Wymon nodded. "Eli's running the ranch right now. How soon can you get started?"

"A week from Monday morning, I'm your man. In the meantime, we'll stay in touch."

He nodded. "I'll plan to drive to Missoula to pick you up. We'll go on the road for the week, pass out our brochures and see how it goes."

"If we manage to influence enough voters to sign our petition, we'll contact the committee and get them doing the same thing."

"It's a plan."

"I've got to get back to Missoula. My wife is waiting for me to take her shopping for some new furniture. I promised. Luckily the store's open until nine."

Wymon smiled. "That's one promise you don't dare break. See you in a week."

He watched Jim leave, but his mind was already on Jasmine. She'd made a promise to Rob Farnsworth she couldn't break, either. Wymon didn't have to like it, but he understood. Jasmine's compassion was part of what made her such an exceptional woman. It showed in every aspect of her life.

After paying the bill, he left the restaurant and headed back to the jewelry shop. When Wymon saw the finished products inside the ring box, his breath caught. "They're perfect."

"That's a real compliment coming from you."

Wymon paid him and put the velvet box in his pocket. He didn't know the moment he would give the ring to Jasmine. They hadn't been seeing each other long enough, but he wanted to be ready when the time came. He knew it was coming just as surely as he knew the sun went down over the Sapphires every night.

More than satisfied with his purchase, he left the store and drove the six miles to the fairgrounds. With the representative's father funding the event, Rob Farnsworth would surely draw a capacity crowd.

In the posters advertising tonight's event, Farnsworth was flashing the smile he was famous for. The last time Wymon had seen the man's face, he'd been snarling.

The lot on the west side of the exhibition hall was already filling up. Wymon decided to park with the rest of the vehicles and sit it out until Jasmine phoned him. While he waited, he called the ranch to talk to his mom who was anxious to know what had happened at the meeting with the governor. Roce had come home to the ranch for the weekend, so Wymon was able to talk to him, too.

While he told him the bad news, a couple of vans from TV stations in Helena pulled in to the reserved parking. He watched for any sign of Jasmine being dropped off by her parents, but by now the place was thick with people and security, making it hard for him to spot her.

It was a good thing he'd come when he did and that he'd driven the Audi. Farnsworth would have recognized Wymon's truck. Better yet, being this close to the hall, Jasmine wouldn't have to walk far to find him after exiting the building.

"So where are you now?" Roce asked him.

Wymon told his brother what was going on. "I won't be back to the ranch until late."

Roce's whistle pierced his ear. "You sure you should be out in the parking lot waiting for her? Farnsworth might come after her and see you."

He took a deep breath. "They haven't been a couple since the crash. If he realizes what's happening tonight, he'll have to deal with it."

"Knowing what he's like, he could make trouble for you and your committee."

"He's already done his best on that count."

"I'm afraid you have a target on your back that has turned personal. Be careful, bro."

Wymon could always count on his brothers watching his back. "I hear you. See you tomorrow."

He hung up and checked his watch. The rally had started. He looked around. The place was crowded, but not so packed that there were lines of people waiting to get in.

At five after seven he received a text.

I'm coming out now. Where are you?

His pulse sped up. I'm in the blue Audi parked in the second row toward the middle.

Wymon got out of the car to watch for her, praying she came out alone.

# Chapter Eight

Jasmine had to admit Rob had delivered a great speech. Now that it was over, his parents had gone up on the platform with him. They waved to her, and she waved back while Buzz took over the mic. She had no idea what they thought about her sitting with the audience instead of supporting Rob onstage, but she couldn't worry about it. Rob would have to make the explanations when this was over.

The crowd rose to its feet and everyone was shouting "Farnsworth" over and over again. This was the moment to escape.

Jasmine moved past four people to reach the crowded aisle. She wove her way through to the back of the room and out the doors. When she stepped outside into the warm air, someone took hold of her arm. "Ms. Telford?"

She whipped her head around to discover the same security guard who'd been waiting earlier to lead her inside the hall before the rally. She removed her arm from his grasp. "What's going on?"

"Excuse me for startling you, but you were hurrying so fast I was afraid I wouldn't catch you in time. Representative Farnsworth asked that you stay here until he could join you."

Before Jasmine could say a word of protest, a tall, sharply dressed man stepped in front of them.

"Please, inform Representative Farnsworth that Ms. Telford has another engagement." Wymon's authoritative voice sent shivers through her. "He needs to check with his manager, Mr. Hendricks, so this problem doesn't happen again. Good night."

After sliding an arm around her shoulders, Wymon walked her to his car and opened the door. She sank on to the seat and looked up at his incredibly striking, familiar face. "If you hadn't come when you did…"

Wymon leaned in and kissed her mouth. "You kept your promise. He didn't keep his. I waited to see if he could be honorable, but he's still out of control, so all bets are off." He made certain her skirt was tucked in before he closed the door and went around to his side of the car.

"I'm so glad you were here," she said softly as he started the engine and backed out of his parking space."

"So am I."

People were leaving the exhibit hall and the parking lot became a swarm of activity. Wymon maneuvered them through the chaos with expertise. After a few minutes they reached the access road to the highway. She was surprised he took the turnoff for Drummond instead of driving into Helena.

"Didn't you want to eat here first?"

"When I saw that security guard grab hold of you, I changed my mind. Don't look now, but we have company following us."

She got a bad feeling in the pit of her stomach. "Is it Rob? He promised me he'd tell his parents everything after the rally."

Wymon shook his head. "Don't worry. It's two security people no doubt hired with his personal funds to keep tabs on you. Hopefully they'll tire of the drive when they realize we're headed all the way to Philipsburg. With tonight's traffic, it'll take a good two hours. We'll see if they're up to it."

"Something's wrong with him, Wymon."

"I agree, but I'm the one Rob is trying to intimidate. He knows he's lost you, which means our coalition's defeat wasn't enough revenge for him."

She frowned. "What defeat?"

"Our proposal for the grizzly reintroduction program was turned down a second time at the state capitol today. We want the governor behind us when we get a bill ready. He says we need to do more work before we bring it to him again. His approval will influence a lot of legislature."

Jasmine hadn't realized. "I'm so sorry, Wymon."

"We'll live to bring it up again another day."

She bit her lip, knowing Wymon had to be a lot more disappointed than he was letting on. "I wish Rob didn't know where I live or work. If I could just disappear for a while, maybe he'd come to his senses and leave us both alone."

He reached for her hand and threaded his fingers

through hers. "I have an idea how you can disappear for a while. We'll have dinner first at this great roadhouse in Deer Lodge where they serve melt-in-your-mouth barbecue. Can you wait that long to eat?"

"Of course."

"Good."

"What if those men stop there, too?"

"It's a free country, Jasmine. As long as they don't bother us, there's no problem."

"I don't see how you can be so calm."

"When Eli and I were on the rodeo circuit, we learned a lot about getting our nerves under control. You have to watch out for the guys who try their intimidation tactics on you to throw you off your game. It was a great place to figure out what fights to pick and what fights to avoid."

"I never thought about the rodeo like that."

"Toly will tell you about guys who try to get inside his head and needle him. That's what Rob is doing right now. He's been in the military and knows how to apply those strategies. But because he's a politician with bigger fish to fry, he'll soon get tired of the game."

Jasmine wanted to believe that, but she'd known Rob long enough to understand his need to win outweighed everything else. She was deep in thought by the time they reached the restaurant.

"I don't know about you, but I'm starving," Wymon said as he ushered her inside. "If those guys followed us all the way, I haven't seen them yet, so don't worry about it."

Once they were shown a table, they ordered a fabulous meal of hickory-smoked ribs, twice-baked southern yams with butter and cinnamon, apple fritters and coffee.

When she couldn't eat another bite, she sat back. "Maybe it's because we had to wait to eat, but I've never tasted anything so good in my life."

His silvery eyes stared into hers across the table. "I'm glad you liked it. Now that we've eaten, I want to tell you about my plans for the next few months. I'm going to be gone a lot."

Her spirits plummeted. "Where will you be?"

"Not so far that you and I can't be together with a little planning. But I'm getting ahead of myself and need to lay the groundwork so you'll understand."

"This sounds serious."

"It is. Our proposal failed because the public hasn't been educated nearly enough to understand our cause. The governor doesn't want this bill to fail, and I believe him. He says we need to do a lot more work, and he's right."

"What more can you do?"

He chuckled and covered her hand. "What every smart politician does. Develop a ground game that covers every inch of Montana and Idaho. It means going door to door, teaching the residents, handing out literature and getting their names on the petition to present to the legislature."

"That's a huge order."

"Yes, and it's going to take time, but I believe it's a fight worth fighting."

"Why does it mean so much to you, Wymon?"

He squeezed her hand before letting it go. "I guess it goes back to my youth. There was a night when my dad took me backpacking up in the Sapphires. Long after the stars came out, he showed me a game trail, and we followed it down to a little lake.

"He took me behind a big tree and told me to be quiet and watch. Throughout the night we saw mule deer, white-tailed deer, elk, a mountain lion and black bears who came to drink. The sight of nature so alive and free was a revelation to me.

"But while I was hunched there spellbound, my father told me a story about the slaughter of the native grizzlies killed off by men for the hell of it." As he talked, her tears started and wouldn't stop.

"'Wymon,' he said, 'seventy to eighty thousand grizzlies once roamed this area. I'd like to see them come back. They should be drinking here, just like the other animals, but they're gone because of man's ignorance. That goes against God's plan, son. Man is supposed to be a steward of the earth, not a killer. I'm afraid we're not doing a very good job.'"

Jasmine wiped tears from her eyes as Wymon spoke his father's words.

"That was all he said before we went back to our camp. I couldn't sleep that night thinking about it."

"You've given me goose bumps."

A sweet smile broke the corner of his compelling mouth. "It does that to me every time I remember our backpacking trip. I wish all the people who oppose our plan could have been there that night to understand what this issue is all about. As I grew older and began studying the issue myself, my father's words seemed to take hold of me."

"It's no wonder, Wymon. I remember seeing a mother grizzly and her adorable cubs when I was a little girl. The thought of thousands of them being killed makes me sick. Your father's words have hit me hard."

"That's the reaction I'm hoping people will feel when they're confronted with the truth about grizzly bears. As you know, the Yellowstone grizzly population has been isolated from its northern cousins, leaving the population at risk of inbreeding. But there have been some sightings of both northern and southern grizzlies in this area. This is a positive sign that grizzlies are closing the gap and reconnecting.

"These first bears drifting into this part of Montana show that connected populations are still possible. The ranching coalition from this area is collaborating with other groups across the region. I'm convinced that in time we can bring about real change."

"That's why you need more funding!"

He nodded. "It takes money to train people to go out and educate the public, not to mention getting signatures for the petition."

"I could help," she said.

Wymon's gaze played over her features. "Do you know what you're saying?"

"What do you mean?"

"For one thing, until a few weeks ago you were

the girlfriend of one of our major adversaries on this issue."

She sat back to ponder his words. "That relationship is over, as you know. The truth is I never did get involved in Rob's politics. Yes, I knew what issues were important to him, but I didn't get into anything with him. Politics were never my interest. I could never see myself campaigning with him. It wasn't the life I wanted. You know that's true."

"I do."

"But what you and I have been talking about is different. No one loves nature and the great outdoors more than I do. I've spent years hiking and horseback riding in the mountains with my family and friends. Hearing your heartfelt opinion on an issue I haven't given any real thought to until now has motivated me to want to do something about it."

A smile lit up his eyes. "You're serious?"

"More than you might imagine."

He leaned forward. "Now you've got a thought percolating in my head. A week from Monday, Jim and I are planning to go door to door to talk to residents about the grizzly issue and gather signatures in support of a new bill we'll have to introduce in January. The whole ranching coalition will be doing the same thing from now until after the holidays. As for next week—"

"Will you be going alone?" she broke in on him.

"Yes. I'd planned to be gone Monday through Friday."

She felt her heart whip up speed. "Would you mind

if I went with you? It's my vacation time. Maybe I could help."

Silence followed before he pulled out his wallet and paid the bill. "Let's drive home and talk about it on the way."

Wymon hadn't said no.

Jasmine got up from the table, and he took her hand as they walked out to the car. She was so excited at the prospect of traveling around with him, she wasn't aware of her surroundings.

After Wymon helped her in and got behind the wheel, he said, "In case you didn't notice, the security people following us took a picture as we were coming out before they drove off."

"That's disgusting. They'll be charging a lot to present Rob with a picture of us this far away from Helena. I can't imagine it being worth anything to him."

"We'll never know, but they're gone now. Let's get back to the subject of your helping me. There's nothing I'd love more, but even though you're on vacation now, you have a little baby at home."

She laughed. "I've been thinking about that."

"So have I. Our coalition group has divided this part of Montana into sections. Jim's area is Missoula County. Mine starts in my hometown of Stevensville, and spreads throughout Ravalli County. With a population of 40,000, it's a lot of ground to cover."

"Your dedication to make this happen is amazing to me. I'd love to be a part of it."

"If you really mean it, I'd like you to spend this

first week canvassing homes with me, provided you stay overnight at the ranch house. My mother always has guests coming and going on business. We'd give Moondrop a stall in the barn and put her out in the corral in the morning. One of the hands would take care of her. In the evening, we'd come home early for dinner and then play with the horses the rest of the time."

To spend five days and nights with him sounded too fantastic to even imagine. "I couldn't impose on your family that way, Wymon."

"You'd be doing me a huge favor. Two people can gather twice as many signatures in the same amount of time. Since meeting you, I've started having fun and want it to continue."

Jasmine never wanted it to stop.

After the loving way he'd talked about his father, she realized his death had to have brought a lot of suffering to Wymon and his family in the last year.

"If you're sure about this, then count me in."

"I've never been so certain of anything in my life." His deep voice resonated in the car and permeated her body.

They drove the rest of the way to Philipsburg involved in their own thoughts. He didn't touch her. When he pulled up in the driveway, he shut off the engine and slid his arm along the back of the seat. His fingers were centimeters from the ends of her hair.

"I'm not going to kiss you, Jasmine, and you know why." She had to stifle a moan because she was aching for him. "Tomorrow evening I'll come for you in the truck. We'll hitch up Moondrop and head for the ranch. Mother will have a guest room waiting for you tomorrow night."

"Wymon—"

"Get out of the car, Jasmine," he whispered urgently.

Once in a while she detected a forbidding sound in his tone that told her he meant what he said. She *did* know why, and it gave her the impetus to act quickly.

"Thank you for everything. Please, drive home safely. I'll see you tomorrow evening."

"I should be here by five thirty, but I'll phone you."

"Okay." She was dying to throw herself in his arms, but Wymon refused to prolong this goodbye. Like she'd told him before, he had more control than she did. After shutting the door, she hurried up the walkway into the house.

All was quiet which meant her parents had gone to bed. On her way upstairs she heard her phone. Someone had texted her. *Wymon?* She raced into her bedroom and sat down on the side of the bed to read it, but it was her coworker Annie!

Vacation couldn't have come soon enough. I'm leaving at six in the morning with Don. We're flying down to Huntington Beach in California to meet his folks. I'll be up packing until at least two. If you're still awake or feel like talking, phone me!

Jasmine had spoken with her after the accident, but so much had escalated since then she couldn't wait to talk to her friend again. Stretching out on the bed, she phoned her.

"Oh, I'm so glad you called me!" Annie exclaimed.

"I was thrilled to get your text. Does this mean Don has asked you to marry him?"

"Not yet, but I feel that's coming."

"Of course it is. You two are crazy about each other."

"What's going on with you?"

"There's so much to tell you, I don't know where to start. For one thing I have a new horse, a little filly named Moondrop."

"You're kidding!"

"Wymon has a friend who breeds horses, and I bought her."

"Before you say anything else, I saw your hunk on the ten o'clock news tonight. He was standing with some other ranchers outside the state capitol building."

"I know. They didn't get the governor on their side yet. Apparently their hope is to gather thousands more signatures and do more research before they go to the governor again for his unofficial approval. Once that is accomplished, they can start the process through the legislature. Wymon isn't giving up!" Jasmine told her friend.

"I tell you, he's in a whole other league of handsome."

"You don't have to convince me," Jasmine said, laughing.

"I also saw your ex on the news at his rally."

"I was there, Annie, but I slipped out after it was over to meet Wymon."

"How did that happen? I thought you broke things off with Rob."

"I did, but I had to keep one last promise to him. Now it's over, and I'm so in love with Wymon, I can't think straight anymore. I'm going to be spending all next week with him."

"No way, girl! Tell me everything while I keep packing."

The two of them talked back and forth half the night. Jasmine had needed this outlet to express all the feelings bursting inside of her. After twenty-six years, she was painfully in love for the first time in her life.

WYMON CAME AWAKE after a deep sleep and shot up in bed in surprise. The clock said ten after nine. He never slept in this late, but last night there'd been a shift in his universe. Thoughts of Jasmine had kept him awake for a long time, and nothing would ever be the same again.

If he hadn't begged her to get out of the car, they'd have stayed there all night. Only the knowledge that he'd be with her for the whole of next week had made it possible for him to let her go.

Before he did anything else, he called his mother and learned that Roce had already left for Missoula.

"We hoped you would come for breakfast."

"I'm sorry. I got home too late and slept in."

"Son? When are you going to relent and talk to

me? I don't mean about the grizzly issue. I tried to get some information out of Roce, but you know your brother. You're both so much alike when it comes to your personal life, I go crazy."

"That's why I'm calling."

"You mean you're going to break the great silence?" She laughed as she said it. Her comment made him smile.

"This woman I helped at the plane crash site has become important to me."

"I knew that weeks ago. I presume the representative is long since out of the picture."

Wymon's mother didn't miss much. His hand gripped the phone tighter. "Not exactly. That's why I could use your help." In a few words he explained the situation without going into a lot of detail. "I'm hoping that while she's at our ranch and gathering signatures with me for the next week, Farnsworth will tire of harassing us."

"Some men never grow up. It's little wonder Ms. Telford had no intention of marrying him. I'd love her to stay here. Solana will get the west guest bedroom ready upstairs. It has the en suite. I'll tell Luis to assign one of the boys to look after Moondrop during the day."

He got to his feet. "You know something, Mom? Our family would fall apart without you."

"Such high praise coming from my number one son has made my day. See you tonight."

*Tonight.*

With an implosion of new energy, Wymon went

downstairs. After a heaping bowl of cereal and a big glass of orange juice, he went into his study. Before he had to leave for Philipsburg, he would plan out his strategy to cover as much ground as possible in the Stevensville area with Jasmine.

Once he had his route all mapped out, he showered and shaved. On his way out to the truck, he carried a box of brochures with the information they'd need to pass out during the week. He put it on the floor of the backseat with a box of snacks he kept on hand.

Before he left the ranch, he phoned Jasmine to let her know he was leaving. "Have you told your folks our plans yet?"

"Yes. What about your mother?" she asked without taking a breath. Something was wrong. It had to be about Farnsworth.

"She's getting everything ready for you as we speak. Now tell me what's happened since I took you home last night."

After a brief silence she said, "Rob sent a message on my cell phone five thirty this morning. The sound woke me up. He didn't write anything. It was a picture of you and me coming out of the restaurant in Deer Lodge. I can't believe this."

"He's hoping to break you down so you'll change your mind."

"But that's not rational."

"His pride has taken a big hit, Jasmine. That's why you and I are going to be busy this next week in a place where he won't be able to find us."

"I'm not so sure about that, Wymon. What if he's

obsessed enough to hire someone to watch my parents' house day and night? They'll see us driving away with Moondrop."

At this point Wymon had to agree it was possible. "Don't worry. I have a plan. I'll tell you about it after I get there."

"Drive safely." He heard the throb in her voice.

"I'll be there soon. Trust me."

After they hung up, he phoned Eli and explained the situation. Before he could even ask him, his brother offered to drive behind him and provide interference if it looked as if someone was casing the Telford home. Eli would do whatever it took to prevent anyone from following Wymon and Jasmine.

The two of them talked strategy in their trucks. Eli would get pictures and anything else necessary if it turned out Jasmine's fears were realized. "This dude has a mean streak like Loco Louis, that bull I once rode. Remember him?" Eli said.

"You're reading my mind."

"If Representative Farnsworth wants trouble, he's found it!"

"Thanks, bro. Sorry to take you away from your family."

"Brianna understands. She's excited another woman will be staying at the ranch this week. Roce told us her new filly is a real honey."

"Libby will go crazy over her."

"My little girl is horse-crazy already."

"You're a lucky man."

"You can say that again. Now that I know your

plans, I'm thinking Brianna and I could do some canvassing for you once we've moved the cows to the other pasture."

"I wouldn't expect that from you."

"Why? We all want to help. Roce is going to do his part when his vacation comes up in a couple of weeks. So is Mom. A lot of work can be accomplished before next January rolls around." Wymon had an exceptional family.

They talked some more, and then Wymon hung up and phoned Jasmine to let her know he was pulling up to the barn. He hadn't seen anyone parked on the street. Eli cruised by and then drove on to scout the area.

Jasmine was already outside and had loaded her horse in the trailer. She came running up to him, a gorgeous sight dressed in jeans and a pullover sweater. "I didn't think you'd ever get here." He caught her in his arms and kissed her until they were both out of breath.

"Come on."

He helped her in the truck and put her suitcase in back. This time it didn't take him long to hitch the trailer to the truck. When he climbed in behind the wheel, he leaned over and gave her another kiss. He couldn't seem to get enough. Neither could she. It went on and on until he found the strength to relinquish her mouth.

"Much as I want to stay here, I'd prefer we get you and Moondrop to the ranch first."

Color filled her cheeks. She nodded and fastened her seat belt.

He knew what was on her mind. "Eli followed me here and will take care of trouble should there be any."

"Did you see anyone outside the house on your way in?"

"Not as far as I could tell." He turned on the engine, and they started down the driveway to the street. There was no sign of his brother. "Eli and I planned the route we'd take home, so he'll follow to see if we pick up someone on the way out of town."

"My parents are worried and angry over this situation. Dad says if anything more like this happens, he's going to talk to the police about it."

"They don't usually do anything unless a crime has been committed. If Rob continues on this course, then the best thing to do is beat him at his own game. Eli and I talked about ways to expose him that will prove embarrassing without calling the police."

"Like what?"

"Like informing him that a leak to the media with a picture of his security men stalking Commissioner Telford's daughter would finish his career. I don't believe for a minute he'd be willing to go that far. But he's intelligent enough to know it could happen if he keeps up this behavior."

"I'm so sorry, Wymon."

"This isn't your fault or mine. Maybe it's the first time in his life that the rich only child and son of prominent oil tycoon Edward Farnsworth III can't have what he wants."

She looked over at him. "Do you think it's that simple?"

"Maybe. Everyone is entitled to one tantrum. What is he? Thirty?"

"Thirty-two. I'm beginning to wonder if he had a problem when he was in the military that no one knows about. He was an officer in the navy and served five years on active duty, but he never talked about his experiences with me. I understand that as soon he came home, he entered politics."

"Too bad all the speculation in the world won't supply the answer. We just have to hope he'll tire of this."

While they were talking, Eli called. "So far no one is following you. I think the dude has realized he'd better not push too hard considering this is an election year. Let's pray that photo he sent to Jasmine is the end of it."

"Amen to that. I owe you, Eli."

"Have you forgotten I'm still in your debt for all the long hours you put in running the ranch while I was absent because of dealing with my divorce? I could never catch up enough to pay you back. Enjoy the ride home."

"You're the best. Tell Brianna thanks for letting me take you away from her and Libby. Talk to you later."

He hung up and darted a glance at the woman who took his breath away every time he looked at her. "All is well and Eli has headed back to the ranch.

Since we're almost to Clinton, would you like to stop at the Stagecoach Restaurant for a pioneer dinner? I'm salivating for their German roast beef and potato pancakes."

"I'm up for anything knowing Rob didn't pay someone to sit out in front of the house and spy on us this weekend."

Wymon's elation had no ceiling as he headed for the turnoff. One whole week with Jasmine to himself… Nothing could have sounded better.

# Chapter Nine

Jasmine had only been inside the entrance hall and living room of the Clayton ranch house the time she'd dropped off the blanket. The high vaulted ceilings were awesome. She felt as if she was stepping back in time when Wymon gave her the full tour. The house had been built with an extensive amount of local stone from the Sapphires combined with distressed barn wood that created its unique design.

She walked on one beautiful Nez Perce rug after another. You could spend hours looking at all the family photos along with the Western memorabilia. Some of the furnishings had to be priceless. Her upstairs bedroom with the fireplace looked out at the mountains. Though it was close to midnight, the silhouette against the night sky was a sight that would be imprinted on her mind forever.

Someone had hand-sewn the exquisite quilt on her four-poster bed. After inspecting the perfect stitching, she looked up at Wymon. "I feel like I've been transported back to another time."

He'd brought up her suitcase and put it at the foot

of the bed. In his Western shirt and cowboy boots, he appeared to be part of the whole fabric. Through the black fringe of his eyelashes, his gaze wandered over her slowly, missing nothing. "I hope you'll be happy staying in this room."

"Who wouldn't be? Your mother has made me feel so welcome! Somehow I thought she'd have dark hair like you, but she's a lovely blonde woman."

"Roce and Toly have her coloring. Eli and I take after our father."

"Well whatever color, she's a wonderful, charming person."

"Mother enjoys having guests."

"I'm very lucky."

"That makes two of us. Since it's late, I'm going to say good-night here. On the way to my house, I'll look in on Moondrop to make sure she's settling in all right. Then I'll come over to have breakfast with you in the morning at seven."

He was leaving her again. Those few kisses in the truck before they'd unloaded her horse had left her more unfulfilled than ever. Did he have any idea what he was doing to her? But she knew it had to be this way, and it *was* late if they were going to get an early start tomorrow.

"Good night, Wymon. I'm so excited to be here."

"If you multiply those feelings by a hundred, you'll begin to know how I feel."

The way he stared at her before going out the door left her burning up inside. She reached for the nearest bed post and clung to it. Her mother's words of a few weeks ago flashed through her mind.

*You're the one who has to live with Rob. If he isn't your be-all, end-all, then the last thing we'd want is to condemn you to an unhappy marriage. One day the right man will show up when you least expect it.*

Jasmine knew in her heart and soul that Wymon was her be-all, end-all. The right man *had* shown up when she'd least expected it. He'd brought her home to meet his mother. If he didn't tell her soon that he was in love with her, too, she didn't know how she was going to function.

Part of her wanted to dash outside to the barn and beg him to stay in there with her for the rest of the night. But he'd brought her here as a guest. If he'd wanted to make love to her all night, he'd have taken them to his house after putting Moondrop to bed.

*Would you have gone with him?*

The answer was easy.

*Yes.*

Jasmine was desperately in love. He'd swept her away, heart, mind, soul and body. There wasn't anything she wouldn't do to be with him. After setting her watch alarm, she climbed under the covers and fell asleep dreaming of him.

She could hardly believe it when her alarm woke her up the next morning. It felt as if she'd just gone to bed, but when she looked at the time, it was six thirty. When she'd packed her suitcase back home, she'd decided that skirts and blouses would be the most appropriate thing to wear when they went door-to-door.

But she'd added something else at the last minute. Yesterday she'd found a store that sold T-shirts with a picture of a grizzly bear mom and her cubs by a stream beneath a snow-capped mountain. She'd bought one for her and another one for Wymon. Maybe he wouldn't think it was a good idea to wear the shirts while they were canvassing, but if not, it would simply be a little present for him.

Once she'd taken her shower and brushed her hair, she dressed in an off-white wraparound skirt and the T-shirt. She slipped on running shoes and hurried down the staircase with his T-shirt inside her tote bag.

Wymon, looking fantastic in tan chinos and an open-necked shirt, was waiting for her at the bottom. When he saw what she was wearing, his mouth broke into a broad smile. "Where did you find that so fast?"

"It's easy if you know where to shop."

"You look gorgeous in it."

"So you think it'll be all right to wear? If not, I'll run back upstairs and change into one of my blouses."

"It's perfect." He pulled her into his arms. "In fact you look good enough to eat this morning." He fused his mouth with hers, and they began devouring each other. But no kiss was long enough or deep enough to satisfy her.

This time it was she who eased away from him first, afraid his mother might walk in on them. They were both out of breath.

"I have a gift for you." She pulled his shirt out of her bag.

Her senses leaped to see the way his silvery eyes

darkened with emotion. Without saying a word, he pulled his shirt over his head, revealing a cut chest with a smattering of dark hair. He placed it on the bannister and put the T-shirt on over his broad shoulders. Jasmine's heart got the workout of its life.

"I don't look as good in this as you do," he said.

*Oh Wymon. If you only knew.* "D-Did you get a good sleep last night?" she stammered.

"No, and you know why." His voice had a slight growl as he cupped the back of her neck and pulled her to him once more in a fiery kiss. "Right now I'd like to carry you upstairs and forget the world."

"I wish you would," she whispered.

She could tell he was trembling. "You shouldn't have told me that."

Feeling braver every second with this man who was such a private person, she brushed her mouth against his. "Why not? It's the truth."

"I'm not sure if you're ready for the answer."

*Wymon, Wymon.* "What more can I do to let you know I'd rather be with you than anyone else in the world? That day you rescued us after the crash, I knew my whole world had changed. The feeling was terrifying and wonderful all at the same time."

"Then you have some idea of my state of mind after I carried you away from the plane and smelled your hair."

*Even then he'd had feelings, too?*

"When I didn't see you at the rodeo, I was devastated. It was very forward of me to approach your brother and tell him about the glasses. But I wanted to see you again so badly—I had to do something to get your attention. Then I was afraid you'd think I was a terrible person."

He sucked in his breath. "If you hadn't done that, I wouldn't be here with you now."

"What made you so hesitant to get in touch with me?"

"At that point I didn't know how involved you were with Rob Farnsworth."

"Since you're the antithesis of a dishonorable man, that's exactly what I was afraid of. Still, I can't help but sense there's something else you're holding back from me."

He held her at arm's length. "When we're alone in the truck, I'll tell you. First, let's eat. Solana's scones are out of this world. Then we'll take Moondrop out to the corral."

WYMON WAITED FOR Jasmine in the truck with the engine running. It warmed his heart to watch the way the filly kept nudging her so she'd give her another treat. Three other horses were already out in the corral for her to get acquainted with. Ron, one of the stockmen, would be keeping an eye on her today until they got back.

"That's all there is for now," he heard Jasmine say through the open window. "Be a good girl while I'm gone."

Her horse neighed several times in protest as Jasmine hurried to the truck and climbed in.

"She's worse than a newborn baby," he teased her.

Jasmine smiled at him as they left the ranch for Stevensville. "I know."

"So how's the mother? Would you rather stay here today? I can turn around and drop you off."

"Don't you dare! She'll be fine. It's you I'm worried about."

"Why?"

"With all these doors we're going to knock on, I don't want some beautiful woman to take a look at you and invite you in for some 'coffee.'"

Wymon threw his head back and burst out laughing, never knowing what would come out of her mouth next.

"Laugh all you want, Mr. Hunk, but I'm a woman, and I know these things."

"Mr. Hunk?"

"Hmm. I saw the nurses at the hospital checking you out. My friend Annie saw you on TV. She said you were in a whole other league of handsome. So now that we're alone with no one to bother us, why don't you tell me why you needed any encouragement at all to phone me after I left the hospital? You have to know that every woman you meet would like to get to know you better."

His hands tightened on the steering wheel. "Those are flattering words, Jasmine, but as you know, what you first see isn't always what you get when you dig a little deeper."

"That's true. It's what the dating experience is all about. You keep trying, sometimes for years, with lots of disappointments."

"In high school I thought I'd end up with the girl I was crazy about. I never considered another option. I'd always worked on the ranch and didn't want another life. When we both started college, I assumed that after graduation we'd get married and build us our own home on the property. But I hadn't counted on Sheila going to Europe on a study-abroad program and falling for someone else."

"Oh, no—"

"While she was in Italy, she met a guy from Hollywood, acting in a film. They spent day and night together. When she came home, she broke up with me. It turns out ranch life wasn't what she wanted, even though she'd come from a ranching background near Stevensville. This guy she'd met offered her a life she couldn't pass up. That was seven years ago. They got married and are still together as far as I know."

Jasmine turned to him. "I can only imagine how much that must have hurt at the time. You'd known her through high school and had no indication that things would turn out differently after college."

"I got over it, but it made me distrustful of my own judgment."

"After the situation with Rob I can relate, but for a different reason. Unlike you, I knew something wasn't right very early in our relationship, but I didn't act on it. I kept thinking everything would become clear if I just gave it more time. Instead it gave him hope and made everything worse. You'd think at the age of twenty-six I would have handled things better."

Wymon shook his head. "Over the years I've dated

various women and have enjoyed their company, but not to the point that I wanted a permanent relationship."

"You probably never gave them a real chance to get to know you. Because if you had, you'd be married by now."

"If I'd fallen in love with one of them, I *would* have gotten married, but it didn't happen."

"How come with me I had to do something overt and then hope you would respond?"

They'd arrived in Stevensville. He drove around the corner of the first residential area he wanted to canvass and pulled to a stop at the curb. After shutting off the engine, he turned to her.

"My reason for holding back with you in the beginning was because I'd learned my lesson with Sheila and the actor she married. It bothered me that once again I was attracted to a woman who in the end wanted an exciting life with a well-to-do politician who could fly her around the country in his own plane. Though I didn't see a ring on your finger, I refused to go through that again."

"But I *wasn't* attracted to his lifestyle, Wymon! Not at all. After a few dates, I was ready to stop seeing him, but another part of me said to give him a chance and not judge him because of his career. Do you honestly think I would have gone to lunch with you that day in the hospital if I hadn't wanted to be with you?"

"I'm not sure I did much thinking that day. What I do know is that I couldn't get you out of my mind."

"I had the same problem and felt so guilty about it. While the man I'd gone flying with was recovering in his hospital room, I lay in my bed down the hall thinking about you. I kept hoping you'd come back to talk to me or call me. When my parents came to pick me up the next day, I told them I wanted to buy you a thank-you gift. I needed to see you so badly, I would have done anything."

"I had no idea," Wymon confessed.

"How could you? As far as you knew, Rob and I had a commitment."

"When Toly told me you'd approached him after the rodeo about the glasses, I had to make a decision whether to ask you to mail them to me, or drive to Philipsburg to get them. We both know it was an excuse to see you again. After you showed up at the ranch with that blanket, I couldn't stay away from you."

"Thank heaven you couldn't," she said softly. "Now that I know your fears, I'm so glad you wanted to see me enough to find out what could be between us. It's what I wanted, too, but I was so afraid you wouldn't try to contact me. I went through agony."

"Agony?" he teased, but deep down her words thrilled him.

"Yes! When I saw your name on the caller ID, I almost had a heart attack I was so happy."

"How many other men have there been in your life who wanted a relationship with you? If you tell me there weren't any, I wouldn't believe you."

"Of course there were men. I had several crushes

on guys in high school, but they burned out fast. In college I had two semi-serious relationships, but my feelings never turned to love. I thought something had to be wrong with me that nothing was working.

"When I happened to meet Rob in my father's office, I was in a bad place because I'd just lost Trixie. As you know, he came along at a low point for me. At first when he pursued me, I was flattered by the attention. It took my mind off Trixie.

"But after a few weeks of dating, I began questioning what I was doing. He was on a political path that drove him. Rob really does want to go all the way. I knew we were both absolutely wrong for each other. He needed a woman who would want to be at his side in all ways."

"You're at *my* side this morning."

"That's different. You've helped me to believe in what you're doing, and I love being with you no matter what we do. Now you know everything about my life." She flashed him a glance. "I'm where I want to be right now."

Right now maybe, but what about the future? That was the operative question for Wymon.

*Let's see how she feels by the end of the week, Clayton.*

He reached around for a bundle of brochures from the box on the floor and split it, giving her half. "Before we get started, why don't you read one of these first?"

She looked adorable as she started to concentrate on the information in front of her.

He got out and pulled two clipboards and pens from the back, each with some petition sheets for those residents who were willing to sign. He'd already downloaded a map of the streets they would cover on his phone. When he got back inside, she turned to him.

"If everyone would study this literature, especially the quotes by John Muir, they would all be converted."

Now was not the time to crush her in his arms. "Knowing that you've become a believer has made my day."

"I think I already was one when I saw that mother grizzly and her cubs years ago. I realize I was little and hadn't learned to fear in an adult way, but that experience has always stayed with me. Since the beginning of time, many wrongs have been committed in this world. We can't fix most of them, but how fantastic would it be to bring the grizzlies back to the home that was once theirs?"

Unable to stop himself, he leaned across to kiss her mouth. "If you'll give that little speech to everyone who's willing to listen, you'll get the signatures we're looking for. While you cover this side of the street, I'll walk across to the other side and meet you at the end of the block. Then we'll cover another section and another and work our way back to the truck."

"Perfect. Whoever gets the least amount of signatures by one o'clock has to buy the other lunch."

"You're on," he said, grinning from ear to ear.

JASMINE GOT OUT of the truck and headed for the first door on her route. She ended up leaving brochures on three front doorknobs because no one was home. At her fourth and fifth house, older people answered and said they didn't have time to talk. But they accepted the brochure with Wymon's name and phone number if they wanted to sign the petition later.

At the sixth door, a teenager, probably sixteen or seventeen, answered in his soccer uniform.

"Hi! I'm Jasmine."

"I'm Mike," he said with a half smile.

"I'm working on behalf of the coalition to reintroduce the grizzly bear back into Montana's Sapphire Mountains."

He sized her up and invited her in the house. She declined and said she hoped he'd show the brochure to his parents. He laughed. "My dad hunts and would probably kill a grizzly if he saw one."

"Why do you think he would do that when it's against the law and they're on the endangered species list?"

"I don't know. So he wouldn't get mauled first?"

This was the very attitude Wymon was up against. "Do you hunt, too?"

"Yup."

"Maybe if you read what the legendary naturalist John Muir said about grizzlies, you'd change your mind."

The teen rested against the doorjamb. "What *did* he say?"

"It's right there."

"Why don't you tell me instead?"

He was being deliberately provocative, but she accepted the challenge. Without consulting the brochure, she paraphrased what she'd read. "Appalled that the grizzlies had all but been wiped out, Muir said, 'The grizzly isn't our enemy. He's simply an equal.'"

"An equal? You've got to be kidding me."

"If you'll read what's there, you might develop an appreciation for grizzlies. Thank you for your time."

As she walked away, he called her back. "I'll take one of those."

Shocked, she handed him one. "I appreciate you listening to me."

She headed for the next house. She had three more houses to go before reaching the corner. The people weren't home, so she left brochures. At the last house she saw a mother come out and put her baby in a stroller. Jasmine introduced herself and asked if she'd be willing to sign the petition.

"Sure. I saw some ads on TV and thought it was an intriguing idea to bring the grizzlies back."

Jasmine thanked the woman for adding her name to the list and hurried to the corner to show Wymon, who was waiting for her. "I got my first signature! Your television ads worked for her."

"That's good to hear." He put an arm around her shoulders and hugged her. "You had better luck than I did. Maybe mine will change. Let's go down this next street and find out."

Between them they covered an average of twenty

houses every half hour. By one o'clock they returned to the truck, having canvassed 160 houses and obtained forty-five signatures, the bulk of them Wymon's. She wished she could have gotten more, but she wasn't complaining because she knew every signature was vital to him.

"Congratulations. I owe you lunch."

Wymon drove them to a drive-thru for burritos and mango freezes. While they ate, she felt his gaze fixed on her.

"What's wrong?"

"Nothing," he answered in that deep voice she loved.

"Forty-five out of 160 isn't a bad percentage."

"I agree."

She swallowed her last bite. "Something's bothering you."

"You've given up your vacation time to help me. I've been greedy wanting you all to myself. It isn't right."

"It's my decision."

"Your willingness to help me means more than you know, but I've made one too."

"That sounds significant."

He chuckled. "In a half day, we've accomplished a full day's work, as much as if I'd been alone. So we're going to go back to the ranch. After we freshen up we'll enjoy the rest of the day. I thought we'd ride up into the foothills."

Jasmine almost jumped out of her skin with excitement. "Much as I'd love that, you need all the help you can get. I'm staggered by the thousands of people out there who haven't heard your message yet."

"It'll get out there slowly but surely." He started the truck, and they headed back to the ranch.

"I don't think you have any idea how much I admire what you and your coalition are trying to do."

"Most people consider it an unnecessary waste of time and money."

"I heard that same argument when my parents took me to Alaska on a cruise after high school. We went out whale watching."

"That's one experience I haven't enjoyed yet."

"It was wonderful. One of the tour directors gave a talk. He said some of us want to conserve whales, but the opposition says 'What's the point'?"

"Our coalition gets that question all the time."

"I learned that today. This guy on the cruise explained that whales play an important role in ocean ecosystems. He said that we should all feel a moral obligation to bring their numbers back because we are the ones responsible for their decline. They have just as much of a right to be here as we do. Your argument for the grizzly repopulation sounds very similar."

"I'm impressed you got that much out of your cruise."

"It was so cool to watch the whales breaching the water. The idea that they could be extinct one day was devastating to me. I feel the same way about grizzly bears and want you to consider me a part of your coalition."

She heard his sharp intake of breath. "I can't let

you do it officially. It will have to be our secret. Otherwise the news would add fuel to the fire if Rob was to find out you were campaigning with me.

"Any association with me and you're going to meet with all kinds of opposition. Our coalition isn't popular with a lot of different groups. The majority of fish and game people consider us a royal pain."

"You're right." There was no one in the world like Wymon. "But you *are* making headway with regular people, Wymon, and you've converted me. Please, use me until my vacation is over."

"I intend to, but I think we should only do half days for the rest of the week. My horse needs the exercise, and Moondrop will love spending time with you. How's the bareback riding going?"

"She's a dream. It's the best way to feel her movements. We're so in sync with each other. I'm going to wait a while to put a blanket and saddle on her."

"It's the only way Jim rides his horses. Has she fought the bridle?"

"No. I played with her gums and massaged them until she opened her mouth and took the bit. She's already used to it."

"You have an amazing way with horses, not to mention all the other ways you continue to surprise me."

While she was basking in the compliment, his cell phone rang. She saw him check the caller ID before he clicked on.

"Wymon Clayton." The conversation didn't last

very long. "I'll pass on the message and she'll come by for it tomorrow. Thank you for calling."

Wymon didn't tell her who had been on the phone and she didn't ask, and soon they were at the main ranch house. He surprised her by driving past it and on up the road where he stopped in front of a small two-story log cabin house.

*His house.* It had to be. She started to tremble.

He turned off the engine before turning to her with a gleam in his eyes. "I believe you've made a conquest. After reading the brochure, some guy named Mike just called and wants to sign the petition, but only if the beautiful curvy blonde named Jasmine returns in the morning before ten."

Heat filled her cheeks. She knew exactly who Wymon was talking about. "He was one of the first people I talked to."

"How old is he?"

"Mid-teens, maybe a little older. If he's serious and has been convinced by the arguments in the brochure, maybe he could be put to work doing a little canvassing for you."

"Don't get any ideas about gathering more signatures with him." Beneath his teasing comment she heard a possessive note that gave her a delicious shiver.

"As if I would."

He got out of the truck and came around to her side. When she would have jumped down, he pulled her into his arms.

"I can't wait any longer to do this." Suddenly they

were kissing with a hunger that wouldn't be appeased. He crushed her against him. No one was around in this secluded spot. The freedom to love him made her euphoric. As her body slid down his hard muscled physique, she felt such a rush of desire, she let out a moan.

"Wymon—"

His ravenous mouth covered hers again, sweeping them away until they were both one throbbing entity. "I want you so badly, Jasmine. You're in my blood. I swore I wouldn't bring you to my house, but I have no control over the way I feel. Help me," he begged.

"I don't want to help you. I want what you want." *I want to love you to the end of time.*

Wymon's body shook. "You say that now."

She lifted her head in surprise. The pain she saw in his eyes shocked her. After all these years he hadn't forgotten what it felt like to be rejected. It caught her off guard because she realized Sheila had been the great love of his life. There was a lot more to his story about her than he'd let on.

He was one of those one-woman men. They were rare in this world. What she would give to be the woman who had such a hold on Wymon's heart that other women who had tried with him failed, and he was still single. That pretty much said it all.

She'd like to tell him all the things she was feeling, but she could see he wasn't ready to hear them. Maybe he never would be. Not with her. Not even if he desired her at the moment. A man could give in to physical desire because it was a fleeting emotion and separate from what the soul truly desired. She knew that and wouldn't get herself into this position again unless he was ready.

"Let's go to the ranch house as planned, then take that ride in the foothills." Jasmine eased herself away enough to get back in the truck and close the door. She was devastated, but she turned a smiling face to him. He'd wanted help. Now he was going to get it. "Come on. We need to make the most of this beautiful summer day. Our horses are waiting for us."

# Chapter Ten

At five to seven that evening, Wymon rode into the barn on Titus. Once in the stall, he removed his trappings and carried them to the tack room. When he returned, he saw Jasmine enter the barn and slide off her horse.

Because of the strength in her legs, she rode like a pro and had the kind of balance that made a saddle unnecessary. Yep, she was an impressive rider. When she turned her body, her horse sensed every motion and followed it.

Up riding among the trees, they moved as one, a picture of trust and coordination in motion. And beauty. Her blond hair combined with the filly's coloring filled his vision until he couldn't look anywhere else. But she didn't look back at him, which didn't come as any surprise.

Before he'd gotten in the truck in front of his house earlier, he'd said something to offend her. It was the last thing he'd meant to do. *Damn* if he hadn't spoken his mind without thinking, and that offhanded remark had chased the magic away.

They'd chatted over the course of their three-hour ride in the foothills, but she was no longer the same woman who would have gone into his house with him earlier.

"Did you like that ride, Moondrop?" she asked her horse as she removed her bridle and led her into the stall. After replenishing her water, she brushed her down.

Wymon joined her. "I think she and Titus enjoyed it as much as we did."

"I do, too," Jasmine murmured. "Thank you for taking us up there."

"It was my pleasure. You must be tired, though. We've put in a big day. Let's go back to the house. Solana's made dinner."

"Did you hear that, Moondrop? Now it's our time to eat. Be a good girl."

After Jasmine gave her horse a hug, Wymon followed her out to the truck, and he drove them down to the ranch house. "That's Eli's truck out in front. It looks like they've come for dinner."

"Oh, good. It will give me a chance to thank him for running interference the other night."

"He was glad to do it."

"But it was a long drive, and I appreciate it."

Wymon walked her inside the house. "Go ahead and freshen up. We should be eating in about ten minutes."

"Perfect."

He watched her hurry up the staircase. Wymon hated the tension between them. It was his fault—all of it—but he couldn't do anything about it until later tonight when they were alone.

After a quick visit to the guest bathroom, he headed to the kitchen where he found Solana and his mother fixing dinner. He kissed his mom's cheek. "Something smells good."

"We've cooked a Texas rump roast."

"Fantastic. Where's Eli?"

"Out on the back porch with Brianna. They've been waiting for you."

"Is Libby with them?"

"No. She's with her mother until Thursday. Why don't you get Jasmine while I tell Eli to come inside."

Wymon walked to the bottom of the stairs and phoned her. But she didn't answer because she was already on her way down. She'd taken off her T-shirt and exchanged it for a printed blouse and a skirt. The need to carry her off to a secluded place was all he could think about.

"Dinner's ready."

"I can smell something wonderful," she said, but she didn't fly into his arms.

He led her to the dining room where he made the introductions. Once they sat down to eat, Brianna wanted to hear all about the plane crash. Eli had filled her in on the situation with Rob, so she didn't delve into anything sensitive.

The conversation soon rolled around to the subject of Libby.

"I would love to have met your daughter," Jasmine said.

Eli smiled at Jasmine. "She's our little cutie. She'll be with us on Thursday and Friday."

For some reason Wymon felt his brother and his wife were excited about something. He looked at his mother who gave him that subtle smile, letting him know something was definitely going on between them.

Wymon ate a fourth yeast roll. "Okay, you two. Out with it—or do we have to live in suspense for the rest of the meal?"

Eli grinned and looked at Brianna, who said something under her breath. "Well, we'd hoped the whole family could be here tonight, but since they aren't, this can't wait. We're going to have a baby!"

Brianna's eyes were shining. "I found out this afternoon. I'm just six weeks. The baby's due in February."

"That's fantastic news!" Wymon got up and went around to hug both of them. He knew that having their own baby would cement their love even more. He eyed Jasmine. "Brianna's brother and his wife are expecting, too. It's an exciting time for the Frost family."

Jasmine glanced at Wymon. "Frost? As in Frost's Western Saddlery?"

"That's my uncle's store," Brianna spoke up. "I stayed with them when I first came here from California."

"Oh! I went there after I left the hospital to buy a thank-you gift for Wymon."

"So *you're* the one." She smiled. "My uncle said

this beautiful blonde woman came into the store and bought one of his most expensive Nez Perce saddle blankets. He said you had excellent taste."

Wymon grinned. "Titus loves it."

"I didn't realize the man who waited on me was the owner. It's my favorite kind of store. I bought a blouse while I was in there, too."

"I bought a lot of things when I used to work for him. Sometimes I still help out, but only on the days when Libby isn't with us."

"How long have you been married?"

"Since March."

"I've been looking at your ring. It's absolutely gorgeous."

"It's a blue sapphire from the Clayton Sapphire Mine in a rare heart-shaped cut. Eli gave it to me on Valentine's Day."

"That must have been the most exciting gift you ever received."

Wymon's mother teared up. "Now there's another gift coming. It's wonderful news! Libby needs a sibling."

"Does she ever!" Eli exclaimed.

Wymon sat back down and turned to Jasmine. "She's going to love your horse."

"If Libby is a horse lover, maybe you'll have to get her a miniature horse. One of the women in the 4-H club raises them. They are adorable."

"Eli?" Brianna said. "Could we get her one?"

"Hold on. One surprise at a time." Everyone laughed.

After dessert, Eli and Brianna excused themselves

to go back to their house on the property, explaining that they needed to make some phone calls to other family members. Before leaving, Brianna turned to Jasmine.

"Why don't you and Wymon come over tomorrow night for tacos?"

"I'd love to."

Wymon didn't say anything, but he gave Brianna another hug. Jasmine offered to help do the dishes, but his mother wouldn't hear of it.

"Dinner was out of this world, Mrs. Clayton. I just want you to know that I don't expect to be waited on all the time while I'm here."

"After helping Wymon do that canvassing, you need waiting on. Why don't you go out on the back porch? It's a lovely evening."

Wymon gave her a hug. "Thanks, Mom." But he had other plans and helped Jasmine with her chair. Instead of walking through the house to the back porch, he headed for the front door. When they'd gone outside, he grasped her hand.

"We need to talk. The only place for that is my truck." He helped her in and took off up the mountainside.

"Your brother and his wife are so sweet. They seem so happy," she said.

"I know Eli is ecstatic. I haven't told you about his first marriage yet. Becoming a father again is already making a new man out of him. They need this baby. Brianna needs it, too, but I'll explain later."

"Where are we going?"

"To a lookout."

A full moon bathed the landscape in light. When he reached his destination, which had a panoramic view of the Sapphire Mountains, he pulled over and turned to her.

"I owe you an apology, Jasmine."

"For what?"

"You don't need to pretend with me."

She lifted her gaze to his. "I don't know what you mean."

"Yes, you do. Ever since we met, I've been fighting my feelings for you. I offended you earlier today and made the situation between us so awkward, I'm surprised you're even still speaking to me. But you were your gracious self at dinner tonight and impressed my family."

She clasped her hands. "When you told me about Sheila and the actor she married after you'd planned your future with her, things suddenly made a lot of sense to me."

He shook his head. "The love I felt for her died years ago. I only told you about her to explain my initial reticence to get involved with you."

"Because you saw similarities in me and my interest in my 'hotshot' pilot," she broke in on him, using his words. "I know."

"We're way past that, Jasmine."

"I agree," she came back in a quiet voice.

"What's going on with me at this point is something entirely different. I shouldn't have asked you to come with me to help canvass. It isn't working.

My mistake. Tomorrow morning I'll drive you and Moondrop back to Philipsburg so you can enjoy your vacation."

Silence enveloped them for a long time.

"Did I do something wrong?" she asked at last. The tremor in her voice broke his heart.

"Of course you didn't," he said.

Jasmine's pain was so acute, she could hardly breathe. "Then you've decided you can't see us together. I get it. Rather than allowing this to drag on in order to let me down gently, you're doing me a favor right now. It's what I should have done with Rob after the first month of dating him."

Her eyes stung with unshed tears. She opened the window to breathe in the night air and gather her wits. "Thank you for your honesty. You're a man who knows his own mind. That's why you're such a successful person. I told you before—you know how to handle any situation, no matter how difficult it is. I admire that."

She hated it that her voice was shaking. "Once you drop me off tomorrow, I promise you won't have anything to worry about where I'm concerned. No surprise visits, gifts or unwanted phone calls. Would you please drive us back to the house now?"

"Jasmine?" his voice grated. "Look at me."

"I'd rather not."

"You honestly don't know the reason I need to take you back to Philipsburg tomorrow?" He sounded strange.

"It's enough that you don't want to be with me

anymore. I don't need to hear all the details. I'm a big girl. I can take it."

She heard a sharp intake of breath. "Can you take it that I'm madly in love with you? Can you take it that all I want to do is go to bed with you and never get up again? Can you believe I wish we never had to say goodbye?" His voice was the one shaking now.

Jasmine jerked her head around in shock. Her heart was pounding too hard to be healthy. He'd finally spoken the words she'd been waiting for.

"Wymon—don't you know how desperately I'm in love with you? I can't function without you now! Why do you think I leaped at the chance to stay here on the ranch? I don't want to be apart from you for a single second."

He shook his head. "You don't understand. I haven't even known you a full month and already I want to marry you as soon as possible. I'm as bad as Eli, who knew he wanted Brianna for his wife within days of meeting her. The only reason they had to wait was to give his ex-wife a chance to bond with her little girl for a few weeks first."

"What do you mean?"

"She had postpartum depression and divorced Eli. She even gave up her parental rights to Libby. But a year later things changed, and she wanted to be a mother again, just as Eli was going to marry Brianna. They separated for two weeks to give Libby time to be with her birth mother."

"I had no idea things were so complicated."

"I thought he was crazy to meet someone and want

to get married that fast after what he'd been through, but I hadn't met you yet."

She smiled. "It must be a gene that runs in the Clayton family. I'm afraid it runs in the Telford family, too." Jasmine reached for him and put her arms around his neck.

"I knew I wanted you for my husband when we were eating in the hospital cafeteria. When I was released, I *had* to see you again and dreamed up that gift so you'd know what was in my heart."

A groan came out of him before he began kissing her senseless.

"I love you, Wymon," she said some time later when he let her take a breath. "I want to be your wife. I'd marry you tonight if I could." She half lay in his arms trying to become one with him.

He covered her face with kisses. "You shouldn't have said that."

"I'm serious. I don't ever want to be separated from you. We could go to the county clerk tomorrow, get a license and have a clerk marry us right there. Montana doesn't have a waiting period. One of my college friends got married that way before her husband was deployed."

"We couldn't do that."

"*I* could. I'd do it in a heartbeat if it's what you wanted."

"It's what I want," he said against her lips, "but your parents adore you and will want to give you away at a big wedding. I've talked with them. You're the light of their lives. To cheat them out of that joy would be unfair."

"We won't cheat anyone, but we'll plan a quick wedding soon. Let's go back to the ranch house and tell your mom first."

"You have no idea how long she's been waiting for this day."

"I already love her for being your mother. She needs to know I can't wait to marry her wonderful son. Tomorrow we'll tell my parents and pick a date."

His eyes burned a hot silver. "You're sure this is what you want?"

"Wymon—what do I have to do to convince you?" she said.

He shifted far enough away from her to reach into his pocket and pull out the most gorgeous ring she'd ever seen in her life. It gleamed green and gold in the moonlight. "This is it, Jasmine." Wymon reached for her left hand and slid it home on her ring finger.

A gasp escaped her lips.

"This is a special green sapphire from our mine. My mother has kept it locked in her safe at the gem shop for years."

"I love it," she whispered. "The wide gold band is so beautiful. It's exquisite. Oh, Wymon. I'm so in love with you I can hardly stand it."

"This stone is the same color as your eyes. When I looked into them at the crash site, I knew something incredible was happening to me."

"I had the same feeling."

After another long, hungry kiss, he started the engine, and they drove back down to the ranch house with her planted against his side, kissing his neck.

"Do you think your mother is still up?"

"Yes. She rarely goes to bed before midnight."

He helped her down from the cab and somehow they made it inside even though their arms were wrapped around each other.

"Mom?" he called to her.

"In the pantry!"

Wymon whispered, "She's doing inventory before she goes shopping in the morning with Solana." They walked into the kitchen. "Jasmine's with me."

"Oh!" In a minute, Wymon's mother came out of the back room. Taking in the sight of them with their arms wrapped around each other, she stared.

"Are you ready for another surprise tonight?"

"Besides the baby?" She smiled a smile reminiscent of Wymon's. "I already know."

"What do you think you know?"

"I don't *think*—I noticed the other day that the spring-green sapphire had disappeared from the safe at the shop. Now that I've seen Jasmine's eyes, it doesn't take a rocket scientist to figure out where it went. May I see it?"

Jasmine couldn't hold back and held out her hand.

"Thank heaven my number-one son had the sense to put it on your finger. That's the perfect setting, and it's right where it belongs. Welcome to the family, Jasmine." She held out her arms, and Jasmine ran into them. They hugged while Wymon stood there, his eyes shining.

"I knew something was going on the second I found out about that rescue. You'd have thought Wymon had been the one in the crash, not you. Though I prayed, I never thought I'd see him so beguiled by anyone. My younger sons always think of him as the solid one who doesn't get fazed by anything."

They all laughed. "My mother noticed I wasn't myself after the crash either," Jasmine confessed.

"Do you have a date in mind?"

"As soon as possible, Mom."

"That sounds like you, but the wedding is for the bride. Do your parents know yet, Jasmine?"

She shook her head. "Wymon's going to drive me back home tomorrow, and we'll tell them then. I can't thank you enough for being so gracious to me while I've been here."

"I haven't been this happy in a long time." She looked at her son, and Jasmine saw tears in her eyes. "I wish your father had lived long enough to see this day. He'd be ecstatic."

They said good-night and Wymon walked her through the house to the staircase. "I don't dare go up with you. I'll see you in the morning at breakfast, and we'll load Moondrop into the trailer. Get a good sleep."

"I won't. I'm too excited for that. I love you." She kissed him several times before dashing up the stairs.

When morning came, she was up with the sun. After packing up her things, she took her bag downstairs and popped into the kitchen where she found Solana.

"Will you tell Wymon I'm going out to the barn? I left my bag in the front hall."

"You don't want breakfast first?"

"Not this morning. I'm not hungry, but thank you anyway."

She hurried out of the house and walked to the barn to load Moondrop into the trailer herself. "We have to leave this morning, but we'll be back soon on a permanent basis, sweetie pie." She kissed her. "You and Titus are going to become the best of friends."

As she was closing the trailer door, Wymon pulled up in his truck. "Solana told me I'd find you here."

"I'm too excited to sleep. I can't wait to tell my parents our news!"

He hopped down and swept her up in his arms. "So you haven't changed your mind?"

"Wymon—"

He laughed that deep laugh she loved, then kissed her thoroughly before helping her into the truck. She noticed it took no time for him to hitch the trailer to the truck. He'd done it enough times to get the knack.

"Did you eat breakfast?"

'No. I thought we'd grab doughnuts and coffee on the way."

"That sounds perfect."

While they drove, she phoned her mom and told her she was coming back with Wymon. "We've had a change of plans. Is Dad there?"

"He's in town at the feed store."

"Do you think he would come home for lunch? We'll be there by then."

"I'll make sure he does, honey."

"Good. We'll see you soon."

She disconnected and snuggled up next to Wymon. "I'm sure she knows something's up," she said, smiling at him. He smiled back, and his eyes were filled with so much adoration that she could hardly keep from throwing herself at him across the seat.

She was engaged, and she and her fiancé were headed to her parents' house to tell them the wonderful news. It didn't sound real to her...but it was. Without a doubt, she would treasure this memory forever.

# Chapter Eleven

Wymon was sure Jasmine's parents had an idea what was going on, but he had his concerns about breaking the news to them. For obvious reasons, they might be skeptical about a wedding happening so fast. When he drove up to the Telford barn two hours later, they were outside to greet them.

After leaning over to give him a kiss, Jasmine got out of the cab without waiting for him. He shut off the engine and climbed out a few seconds later. She held out her hand to him, and they walked over to her folks.

"Mom? Dad? Last night Wymon asked me to marry him. We want to get married right away. He gave me this sapphire engagement ring from their mine. Isn't it gorgeous?"

"Honey!" her mother cried, and they hugged.

Mr. Telford flashed Wymon a broad smile and patted his shoulder. "Congratulations. I've known how our daughter felt from the moment we found out you'd rescued her at the crash site."

"It's true, and we're thrilled you're going to become a part of our family!" Jasmine's mother gave Wymon a big hug. "Let me take another look at that ring."

He gave Jasmine a kiss on the cheek. "While you do that, I'll unload Moondrop and take her in to her stall for some water and food."

Her father helped him, and they walked the filly inside the barn. "I love your daughter, Mr. Telford. I swear I'll do everything in my power to make her happy."

"You already have, son."

"But I'm sure you're concerned that this has happened so soon after her breakup with Rob Farnsworth."

"Jasmine was never in love with him. It's a shame he proposed to her right before the crash and she had to turn him down, but that has nothing to do with you."

"I agree, but it's gotten ugly since he found out about us. One of the reasons I asked Jasmine to do some canvassing with me was so she could get away where he couldn't find her for a while. But last night I realized I had to tell her how I felt. So we're back for your blessing."

"You've got it," Jasmine's father said, smiling at him.

"That means the world to me. My mother and family will go along with whatever we plan, but Jasmine's your only child, and I want this to be her day."

"You're a good man, Wymon. Let's go in the house and we'll talk."

On the way back, Wymon undid the hitch of the trailer. Then they entered the kitchen where Jasmine was helping her mother make sandwiches and iced tea. The four of them sat down at the kitchen table to eat.

Jasmine eyed her parents. "We've talked for hours and think we should get married quietly in front of the family so Rob doesn't know anything about it. Once the election is over in November, we'll have a big reception, and it won't matter that the news is out."

Her father nodded. "I think it's wise that you're considering Rob's feelings. If Wymon were any other man...but he and his coalition are the ones Rob has targeted during this campaign season. *And* he's the man who rescued both you and Rob at the crash scene."

"I agree," her mother said. "It would be much better to keep the news from him for the next few months. That's very kind of you two to help him preserve his pride while he's still this vulnerable and hurting."

"We don't know what else to do. I was telling Wymon I'll change my hours and go back to work tomorrow until our wedding day. Then I'll take my vacation so we can have a honeymoon. We're thinking the end of July."

"That's soon," her father quipped. "Less than two weeks away."

"But the date works. His brother Toly would be able to fly home that day and get back to Oklahoma in time for the Sunday night rodeo. Of course it will depend on Minister Logan. I know it isn't very far away, but since this will be for family only, there shouldn't be a problem."

"Do you want to get married here at the house?"

"Yes," she said after looking at Wymon. "Much as we'd love a ceremony at the church, we can't take the chance of word getting out. Would that be all right with you, Mom?"

She looked at her husband. "We wouldn't want it anywhere else."

"If you'd like one suggestion from your old dad, why not plan to say your vows again in November at the church in front of the whole world? That way we'll all have the wedding of our dreams."

Jasmine's face let up. "That's absolutely perfect!" She jumped out of her chair and ran around the table to hug her father.

They all talked a few more minutes before her father excused himself to get back to work. He squeezed Wymon's shoulder on the way out. "We couldn't be more pleased, son."

"I feel the same way. I'm afraid you'll be seeing a lot more of me from now on."

"Wymon," her mother said. "Don't you know this is the day every parent waits for? To see their child marry their be-all, end-all?" She looked at her husband. "That's what I did. I'll walk you out to the car, darling."

Once they were alone, Wymon pulled Jasmine

down on his lap and rocked her for a moment. "I don't know if I can wait."

"I know I can't. Oh, Wymon—we're getting married!" She burst into happy tears, and he kissed her silly until his desire for her brought him to his feet. He crushed her body against him. "That's why I've got to go home now, sweetheart."

"No-o-o."

"If we're going on a honeymoon soon, I need to work my head off. Once I'm back in Stevensville, I'll keep gathering signatures through the coming weekend. On Monday, Jim'll be joining me."

"I'll go back to work first thing in the morning, too. This will be our longest separation."

"But then we'll be together forever. Do you know where you want to go for our honeymoon?"

"Wherever you want. Call me from the truck and we'll plan it out."

"You haven't even been in my house yet."

"It's better this way. Once you take me inside, I'm never coming out again."

"You've got that right. Kiss me once more, sweetheart."

On Friday Jasmine came home from work excited to talk to her parents. She'd heard from Annie whose boyfriend had also proposed. They were getting married next month.

While she was pulling in the driveway, her phone rang. When she saw that it was her mom on the caller

ID, she didn't bother to answer because she'd be seeing her in less than a minute.

As Jasmine got out of the car, she noticed an unfamiliar Lexus parked in front of the house. She decided it was someone who'd come to see her father. Full of news, she hurried inside. Tomorrow she and her mother were going to drive into Missoula to find her a wedding dress and veil to wear at both ceremonies. She also planned to buy a wedding band for Wymon.

"Mom?"

"In the living room, honey. We have guests."

*We* have guests?

The double doors off the living room were ajar. When Jasmine pushed them open, her heart plunged right through her feet to the basement of the house.

*Mr. and Mrs. Farnsworth.* They were seated on the couch drinking iced tea.

Her mother got up from the chair near the fireplace. "Rob's parents dropped by to talk to you. I'll be in the kitchen to give you some privacy."

After her mother slipped out of the room, Jasmine held on to the matching chair on the other side of the hearth. She felt ill. "Has Rob had a relapse since the accident? Is that why you're here?" It was the only reason she could think of for their unexpected appearance.

His mother leaned forward. "His concussion has healed, but he's been in a bad way since the rally in Helena. We don't understand why you weren't up onstage with the rest of us."

Oh, no. "You mean he didn't explain?"

Mr. Farnsworth shook his head. "You're the only one who knows what's going on with him. I've talked to Buzz, but he hasn't been able to enlighten us. We're very worried about him."

"What has he told you about us?"

"That he's in love and plans to marry you."

Their sincerity caused a groan to escape her throat. She felt terrible for them, but this wasn't her problem to solve. "We're not getting married. I'm sorry you've driven all the way here for answers, but I can't help you. This has to come from Rob."

"What are you saying?" his mother asked.

"Only that he should be the one to explain why a marriage between us won't work."

His father grimaced. "Come on, Nadine. This was a wasted trip."

They got up and left the room. Jasmine opened the front door for them. They both saw her engagement ring before walking out to their car. That was another shock.

Jasmine shut the door before burying her face in her hands. In a second she felt her mother's arms go around her.

"Oh, Mom. Rob still hasn't said a word to his parents about us. I told them we weren't getting married and that he would have to be the one to answer their questions."

"If they saw the ring Wymon gave you, then they've figured things out."

"They did see it, but didn't say anything."

"When they showed up here, I took them into the living room and went back to the kitchen to fix some iced tea for them. While I was in there, I called to warn you, but you didn't pick up."

"I know. I heard the phone, but I'd just driven in the driveway and knew I'd be talking to you any second. They must have a new car, because I didn't recognize it. But none of it matters now."

"No, it doesn't. They shouldn't have come. You were never engaged to him. It shows they'd do anything for him. I have the feeling this is a lesson he needs to learn the hard way. As for you, honey, you're about to embark on a new life and can put this behind you."

Jasmine wiped her eyes. "You're right, but I've got to phone Wymon and tell him what happened." She hugged her mother, then dashed upstairs to her room.

To her frustration, she got his voice mail. He was out canvassing. No doubt he was in the middle of a conversation with a voter. She left a message to call her as soon as he could.

After changing into jeans and a top, she went out to the barn. A ride on Moondrop would settle her nerves until she could talk to Wymon.

WYMON PARKED IN front of his house at ten to ten before checking his messages. There were a lot of them. He always looked for Jasmine's first, but this time the call from his mother took precedence. She'd said to phone him immediately.

Before he went inside, he rang her. "Mom?"

"Thank goodness. Are you home?"

"Just drove up."

"Well, don't go inside yet. You have a visitor who's been waiting for you for over an hour. I have the feeling he'll wait here all night until you show up."

He didn't have to guess. *Farnsworth.* Maybe Jasmine had phoned to warn him. "I'll be right there."

"The representative is in the living room."

"Thanks for the heads-up."

With lightning speed, he drove down to the ranch house. On the way he phoned Jasmine.

"I'm so glad you called," she blurted.

"What's wrong?"

"Rob's parents were here when I got home from work this evening." His eyes closed tightly. "They wanted to know why I wasn't up on the stage with them at the rally. Rob didn't tell them the truth about anything."

That didn't really surprise Wymon.

"I explained that we wouldn't get getting married and told them they would have to talk to their son for answers. As I was letting them out the door, they saw the ring on my finger, but didn't say anything. It was awful."

"I believe it. Since their visit to your house, they must have told Rob what they saw because he's waiting for me at the ranch house as we speak."

"No."

"It's all right. Mom has warned me. I'll handle this and phone you as soon as he leaves."

"I'm afraid, Wymon. His parents were so upset."

"His fear of letting his parents down has caught up to him. Frankly, I'm glad this happened. We've bent over backward not to hurt him, but it needed to come out for all our sakes."

"Please, be careful. I don't know how stable he is," she said.

"Don't worry. I've got a whole ranch to back me up, not to mention my brother next door if I need him. But to be honest, I don't think this amounts to anything more than having lost something important to him for the first time in his life.

"He's a good man, but it's a hard lesson to learn if he's lived this long without tasting defeat. At least we know his parents finally confronted him and got through to him. That's a start in the right direction, don't you think?"

"You're so levelheaded, you're scary, Wymon Clayton."

"Is that good or bad?"

"I'll tell you after you phone me and let me know you're alive and well."

He clicked off and headed into the living room of the ranch house. Farnsworth was standing in front of a wall of family pictures, studying them.

"Mr. Farnsworth. If I'd known you wanted to see me, I would have come sooner."

Rob's head jerked around. He stared at him for the longest time. "I wasn't sure I'd be welcome."

Wymon took a deep breath. "Why don't we sit down?"

He remained standing. "What I have to say won't

take long. I've come to apologize for my parents who, without my permission, paid a call to Jasmine earlier today. They've made my business their business all my life, but this was one time they went too far."

Agreed.

"They loved Jasmine the first time they met her, and my father has let me know repeatedly that she's the woman I should marry. The fact that I was in love with her and felt exactly the same way made everything perfect, except for one thing. Jasmine was never in love with me. I'd hoped in time it would happen, but it never did."

Rob's confession took a lot of courage. Wymon couldn't help but admire him. "I felt the same way about a woman back in high school and college. To my shock, she came home from a trip to Europe and told me she was marrying someone else. I went through hell for a long time."

"That's where I've been. But when my parents told me they'd been to see her, something snapped inside me. I told them there wasn't going to be a marriage, and we needed to get over it."

At last.

"What I'm trying to say is, I've behaved like a jealous, lovesick school boy, and I'm not proud of it. I hope the day will come when Jasmine will forgive me for sending her that picture of you two on her phone. That was inexcusable."

"She knew how much you were hurting and has already deleted the picture. It's forgotten."

"Jasmine's an exceptional person, but you already

know that. The fact that you and I are on opposite sides of the same issue just fueled my anger."

"I get it," Wymon murmured.

"That was wrong of me, especially when you were the person who helped save our lives at the scene of the crash. My folks told me they saw an engagement ring on her finger. It couldn't be anyone's but yours."

No more secrets. "We're getting married next week."

He nodded. "I hope you'll be very happy. I mean that sincerely."

"I believe you." Wymon extended his hand and they shook on it.

"This doesn't mean I won't be fighting just as hard against the idea of a new grizzly population. I just don't see the reason for it, but I respect the fact that you do. There'll be nothing personal about my campaign from here on out."

"I appreciate that, Rob, and I wish you the very best. I'm sure if you phone Jasmine tonight and tell her what you've told me, you'll always have a friend in her."

"Thank you. I will. Please, tell your mother I'm sorry I imposed this long."

Wymon walked him to the front door. "She's used to business going on at all hours."

"Isn't that the truth."

After Rob left, Wymon went back into the living room to call Jasmine.

"Wymon?" She sounded frantic.

"Relax, sweetheart. All our worries are over. He

knows we're getting married, and all is well. To be honest, I like the guy. He's really very decent. I have a feeling he's going to be calling you in a few minutes. Phone me when it's over and we'll talk. I love you."

ON WYMON'S WEDDING DAY, Toly came running out of the Missoula airport and climbed in the backseat of Wymon's car, hugging him around the neck.

"Hey—you're cutting off my breathing."

"You'll live. Bro—I never thought I'd see the day you'd get married before me or Roce."

"He caught Eli's bug," Roce said over his shoulder.

"That means you're next. It might even happen before my finals in December."

"No way." Roce shook his head.

"Want to make a bet? Where's Eli, by the way?"

"He's taken Brianna and Mom to Jasmine's house. They're waiting for us."

Toly finally sat back so Wymon could breathe. "Since you're not worried about hurting the representative's feelings, how come you're not getting married at the church?"

Roce turned toward him. "Because big brother here couldn't wait a second longer."

"I can see why," Toly remarked. "She's drop-dead gorgeous. Mills is still in mourning."

Wymon smiled. "She's a lot more than that. We'll do a big wedding in November to give everyone time to make plans and come. This little ceremony is just for us."

"Hey, Roce—how come you're letting him drive?"

"Wymon doesn't trust me to get us there in time. You know what's funny? He was late picking me up at the vet hospital. How come?"

"I had to search for our wedding license at the last minute," Wymon grumbled. "We went to get it the other day, and I forgot where I put it."

His brothers laughed and cracked jokes about nervous bridegrooms all the way to Philipsburg.

When Wymon pulled up in the Telfords' driveway, the only cars he saw were Eli's and what he imagined was Minister Logan's. His heart picked up speed as they got out of the car.

Jasmine's father met them at the front door and showed them into the living room, which had been reserved for men only. The ceremony was taking place on the back patio.

"My wife has the women sequestered. I'm to give each of you a small gardenia for your lapels. Gardenias are my daughter's favorite flower."

Wymon had trouble pinning his on. Toly came over to help him. "I'd like to think Dad is looking on."

Wymon had a hard time swallowing. "I hope so. Thanks, Toly. Thanks for coming on such notice."

"I wouldn't miss your wedding for anything."

Wymon handed the minister their license, but he was getting antsy waiting for things to start. He checked his pocket for the wedding band and handed it to Roce.

His brother smiled at him. "Thanks for the honor."

He gathered his brothers. "You guys are the best."

Eli handed him an envelope. "This is from all of us. You only get one honeymoon."

"Thanks, but you guys need to keep your money. We'll take a small one after our wedding in November. For the time being we're just going to stay on the ranch."

"You'd better look inside," Eli told him.

Wymon did his bidding. To his shock he found two round-trip tickets to St. Lucia in the Caribbean for ten days, all expenses paid. There was also a voucher for a night's stay at a hotel in Missoula for that night. Their flight left in the morning.

"Our mom and Jasmine's mom have packed your bags. You're all set," Eli told him.

Toly's brows lifted. "Ten days on a beach, lying there beneath the palm trees with the love of your life in your arms? If you don't take advantage of this, you're not the brother I thought you were."

"He's right," Roce broke in. "Not too long ago I told you there was a reason you happened to come upon that crash site. You've worked so damn hard for so long, it's time you allowed us to do something for you."

Too touched for words, Wymon was still pondering what to say to his brothers to thank them when he heard a woman's voice say, "Everyone?"

Jasmine's mother, dressed in a pale peach suit with a gardenia on her shoulder, stood in the entrance to the living room. "If you'll all come out to the patio."

Wymon put the envelope in his pocket and followed his brothers to the back of the house where chairs had been placed in a semicircle. Brianna and his mother were wearing hyacinth-blue dresses with flowers on their shoulders. His mom's smile told him how happy she was this day had come.

The minister stood before them. In a minute there was a hush as Jasmine walked out onto the patio like a princess, holding on to her father's arm. Wymon could hardly breathe.

She was a vision of gold hair and oyster silk that swept the tiles and a lace mantilla that fell to her shoulders, half hiding her lush green eyes. Her gaze sought Wymon's. The love he saw there filled his soul to overflowing.

"Jasmine? Wymon? If you'll come forward and clasp hands in front of me."

He felt as though he was in a dream as she seemingly floated toward him. He twined his fingers with hers. Their heartbeats merged. Suddenly the ceremony he'd been waiting for had begun. They repeated their vows, but none of it seemed real until the minister said, "Wymon? Do you have a token for your bride?"

Eli came forward and handed him the wedding band. He turned to Jasmine and slid it next to the engagement ring he'd given her. Then the minister asked, "Jasmine? Do you have a token for your groom?"

She removed a gold band from her least finger and fit it on his ring finger, pushing it home. His heart leaped at the sight of it.

With a beaming smile Minister Logan said, "I

now pronounce you man and wife. What God has joined together, let no man put asunder. You may kiss your bride."

*"Jasmine,"* he whispered against her lips before covering her mouth with his own. He forgot they had an audience. This was his wife he was kissing. Only a little over a month ago he hadn't even met the love of his life and wondered if he ever would.

"Hey, bro—" Toly whispered behind him. "If you two are going to make your plane, you'd better break this up and give everyone a chance to congratulate you."

When he finally let her go, his brothers took turns hugging her and welcoming her into the family. Two hours later they'd eaten and celebrated. Then Jasmine changed into a blouse and skirt while Wymon removed his tux and put on chinos and a button-down.

After Wymon had hugged his mother one final time, they went out to the car with their bags. They shouted goodbye, and Roce drove them to their hotel in Missoula.

He got out at the hotel entrance to help them with their bags. "Don't worry about anything on the ranch while you're gone. We've got it covered."

"I know you do. I owe you for everything." Wymon gave his brother another big hug and rushed his bride into the hotel lobby. Roce was keeping Wymon's car until their return.

This trip hadn't been part of the script, but Wymon found he was excited to go to a place neither of them had been to before. The whole day still had a surreal feel about it.

They got their card key and went to their room on the third floor. Every day and night since he'd met Jasmine, Wymon had wanted to get her alone like this and never let her go. When they went inside the hotel room, it hit him that the time had finally come.

Jasmine watched him put their bags down. When he turned to pull her into his arms, she all but leaped into them. Her need to be alone with him like this was all that mattered. He carried her over to the bed and laid her down, smoothing the hair away from her face.

"You're the most beautiful sight I have ever seen. I love you so much, my wife."

"I adore you, Wymon. You're my everything. You know that, don't you?"

Moaning, he devoured her mouth with his, whisking her away to a world she could never have imagined. He did things to her, thrilling her in such incredible ways she lost herself in a sensual ecstasy impossible to describe. She'd known his tender side, but his passion shook her to her foundation and took them both to heights she never imagined possible.

Throughout the night they found new ways to love each other. Sometime before dawn, they finally went to sleep so they would get a few hours of rest before they had to fly out.

Jasmine moaned in protest when the front desk sent them their wake-up call.

"No-o. I don't want to move from this spot."

"My biggest worry is how to keep my hands off you while we're on the plane."

"I plan to sit on your lap."

His laughter sent a thrill through her as she thought to herself: *This is only the beginning.*

## Chapter Twelve

The Bahamas with Jasmine had been a living fantasy Wymon would remember for the rest of his life. But when he drove her to his house, which was now *their* home, and he saw the sun going down over the Sapphires, a feeling of wholeness enveloped him.

He got out of the car and came around to open her door. She was a radiant, sun-tanned vision of beauty. "Welcome home, sweetheart."

"*Home...* It seems like I've been waiting for this forever!"

He drew her out of the seat and carried her up the stairs to the front porch. She kissed him all the way with an eagerness he craved. Somehow he managed to unlock the door and carry her over the threshold. After shutting the door with his heel, he took the stairs to his loft, his aerie where he could look out on to his private Eden.

He carried her over to the floor-to-ceiling window so she could take in the majesty of the mountains at this perfect time of night. It was high summer in the Sapphires. When he lowered her to the floor,

Wymon drew her back against his chest and wrapped his arms around her. Together they feasted on the glorious sight before them.

"For years I've stood here watching twilight creep over the land, turning the pinks to lavender, then purple, just like it's doing now. Only this time you're with me to complete the landscape of my life," he said.

She turned in his arms and stared into his eyes. "Besides being the most wonderful man who ever lived, there's a poet in you, Wymon. You're in tune with nature in a way I've never experienced with anyone else.

"Seeing the way things look through your eyes inspires me whether you're talking about the moons on my filly's coat, or the waves on the beach undulating like cloud formations before a storm. Sometimes when you tell me about the tenderness of a mother grizzly playing with her cubs, or a she-wolf loving her babies, it brings tears to my eyes, you know that?"

She slid her arms around his neck. "How did it ever happen that you were there in the mountains that day when I needed you?"

He drew in a deep breath. "Roce said it was meant to be. I believe it now because you're the miracle I've waited for such a long time."

Unable to hold back, he carried her over to the bed and followed her down, needing to feel her beautiful body against him. "I want you to stay there. Don't move until I get back. I'll bring our things in from the car."

With one last plundering kiss, he hurried out of the room and down the stairs. On his way out, he walked into the kitchen and saw that his mother had bought them groceries. He'd thank her later and went out to the car for their bags.

When he returned to the bedroom, he discovered his wife in the shower. He'd told her not to move, but this was much better.

He whipped off his clothes and stepped inside the en suite. Jasmine was washing her hair. Moving into the stall behind her, he said her name to warn her.

"Oh—"

"Need some help?"

For the next little while they brought each other to new, dizzying heights of ecstasy. Then he wrapped her in a fluffy towel, nuzzling her neck. "Mother brought us food if you want some."

She shook her head. "That was so kind of her, but I'm not hungry. But I'm sure you are, so eat if you need to."

"I'd rather just go to bed."

"That's what I want to do. I've been dying to sleep in my husband's arms, in *his* bed in *his* house."

"Our house, sweetheart. From now on, Wymon and Jasmine Clayton live here."

He helped dry her hair with another towel, and they climbed under the covers. She sounded sleepy when she said, "During the flight I wished we'd had our own private sleeping compartment. I don't know if I can take long flights with you very often. It's too hard on me."

One of the things he loved most about his wife was her passion, which equaled his own. A woman with less fire would never have held him. While they'd walked along the beach in St. Lucia, they'd talked about the children they wanted to have. His heart had leaped when she told him she'd love to start a family right away. To have a baby with her would be the fulfillment of all his dreams, so they weren't doing anything to prevent getting pregnant.

Jasmine had arranged with her supervisor at the university to work out of the extension office in Stevensville. Tomorrow they'd bring Moondrop home. No man could be as happy as he was tonight. With her beautiful body merged with his, he wanted for nothing.

"Sweetheart?"

Wymon was calling to her, but he'd just come down from the pasture expecting to find her dressed for the Halloween party at Eli's. Roce was coming, too.

But the waves of nausea that had been assailing her for the last two weeks had gotten so much worse. Jasmine had gone to Brianna's doctor in Stevensville without telling her husband. Her joy in learning she was pregnant made the discomfort worth it. At least that was what she'd told herself until today. The doctor had given her medicine, but it probably wouldn't kick in for another day or two.

"I'm still in the bedroom!" she replied.

He came bounding up the stairs and into the room,

sweeping her into his arms as he always did. But she couldn't respond and lay back on the mattress, limp.

"Jasmine—" He groaned. "You're so pale. Something's wrong."

The terrified look on his face revealed the degree of his anguish. She'd wanted to surprise him in a special way tonight. Jim Whitefeather's wife had loaned her an authentic Nez Perce deerskin dress and a cradle board to put on her back. Wymon would be sure to notice the significance of the costume, and she thought it would be a fun way to break the news.

But she'd only gotten dressed as far as her slip before she'd broken out in perspiration. Wymon's war bonnet, borrowed from Jim, was lying on the chair.

Wymon examined her one more time. "I don't like the look of you at all. Let's get you to the hospital."

"I've already seen my doctor."

"What doctor is that?" He sounded panicked.

"My new OB."

"Your *OB*? Jasmine— You're pregnant?" he cried.

"Yes, darling. It's the best news. We're going to have a baby, but the nausea—" She broke free of his arms and ran to the bathroom where she was sick for the second time today.

He came in and held her, then helped her over to the sink to brush her teeth and wash her face. Wymon stood by with a towel to wipe her face, then he helped her walk back to bedroom.

"I'll call Eli and tell him we can't make it. Once he knows why, he'll understand."

"No. We'll go, but just for a little while. I don't

want to spoil their party. Brianna and your mom have gone to so much trouble already. Some of the neighbors will be dropping by for trick-or-treating. I wouldn't dream of letting them down."

"That doesn't matter, not with you this sick."

"I'm okay—I can handle it." He didn't look as if he believed her. It gave Jasmine her first inkling of what life was going to be like from here on out. He'd watch her like a hawk and worry about her constantly over the next seven months of her pregnancy. Her husband had been so happy for so long. Now he had a son or daughter coming, and it had aged him ten years in one night!

When they'd both gotten dressed, she grabbed hold of his arms before they went downstairs.

"Wymon—I'm not dying," she said. "And I'm not going to die! After the medicine the doctor gave me kicks in, I'll be much better. This will pass. I understand Brianna had her moments, too, and she's fine now that she's farther along."

"I've never seen you go that color," he said. "You don't know what ran through my mind when I saw your face. You didn't even look like that after the plane crash."

"It's because I wasn't carrying Wymon Clayton's baby then," Jasmine teased him. "This child is so precious that it wants us to know it's on its way big-time." She flashed him a smile. "Just think, one day he or she will see your dream for the grizzlies to return to the Sapphires come to fruition. Keep that thought in mind every time you start to get nervous for me."

He cupped her face in his hands. Those silvery eyes took in every inch of her. "You're so brave. I'm in awe of you. I saw your courage when I realized you'd climbed out of that broken plane to save Rob."

"Have you forgotten your bravery? You saved me and Rob and prevented a tragedy by calling 911 when you did. I'm so proud to be carrying your child, you have no idea. Now let's hurry to Eli's while I can still function. But you'll have to make the announcement because I'm feeling weak."

"Let me help you get dressed." After they were ready he carried her downstairs to the car, and they drove to Eli's home. It was decked out with Halloween decorations. There was one jack-o'-lantern for every member of the family. Eli must have spent hours carving the intricate designs.

Wymon's mother had come dressed as a frontier woman sporting an Annie Oakley hat and a long rifle. Luis and Solana wore matching flamenco outfits and looked as if they'd dropped in from southern Spain. Brianna had dressed as a pregnant Sleeping Beauty. Eli was her Prince Charming.

Roce stole the show with a replica of Prince John's costume and wig from Robin Hood. But to his mother's chagrin, he hadn't shown up with a girlfriend. Little Libby ran around wearing a witch costume Brianna had made with a tall pointed hat and a wand.

"Oh, Libby," Jasmine cried. "Look at you—Wymon,

isn't she adorable?" But when she glanced up at him, he was staring at Jasmine. "Wymon?" she prodded him.

"Yes, she's adorable."

"What's wrong?"

He pulled her close and whispered, "I just had a vision of our little girl in a witch costume one day."

"I had my own vision, but it was of a little boy in chaps and a cowboy hat, looking like his dad."

"Hey, you two—" Eli spoke up. "What's all the whispering about?"

She waited for Wymon to speak.

"Family? We're going to have a baby, but Jasmine has morning sickness. If she gets sick again like she did earlier, we're going to have to leave."

Everyone shouted in delight and hugged both of them.

Libby tugged on Wymon's jeans. "Baby?"

He got down on his haunches and kissed her. "Just like the one Brie is going to have."

"Let's get Toly on the phone and tell him!" Roce suggested. "The news ought to fire him up to take the national championship in December."

But Eli kept staring at Wymon. "Are you okay, bro? You look a little pale in that headdress."

"I'm still getting used to the idea that I'm going to be a father."

A grin spread across his face. "Boy, are you in for it now."

"I found that out earlier tonight and am still trying to recover."

He patted Wymon on the shoulder. "Welcome to the daddy club."

"Did you hear that, Roce?" their mother said to her son so everyone could hear.

No matter how sick Jasmine felt, she laughed out loud. Mrs. Clayton walked over to Jasmine and gave her a big hug. Then she pulled her aside.

"I'm so happy for you, I could cry for joy. Just so you know, of all my sons, Wymon is the most like his father. His dad worried constantly while I was carrying our number-one son. He treated me like I was the sacred holy grail. You'll get used to it." Jasmine chuckled again because everything she'd said was so true.

"No matter how worried your husband gets, just smile and get him to do some project for you. Keeping him busy is the key. And one more thing—it's good that Eli has already been through this. He'll help Wymon at the right moments. Brianna's baby will be here first, so that will help prepare my oldest boy."

"I love you," Jasmine said, throwing her arms around her mother-in-law who'd raised the four finest sons in the West.

"Jasmine?" At the sound of her husband's voice, she turned toward him. The stress lines on that handsome face of his made him look drawn. "Let's sit down. If you can't eat, shall I get you a cola?"

She didn't want anything, but after remembering what his mother had just told her, she said, "I'd love one. Get some food for yourself, too, while you're at it."

He led her to the sofa in the living room. "Will you be all right?"

Good grief. "I will be after you bring me a drink."

"I'll be right back."

His mother glanced at Jasmine, and they both shared a conspiratorial smile. Soon Libby toddled over and sat down next to Jasmine. She lifted her dress to show her the crazy red-and-white striped stockings that Brianna had bought her. "See my stripes?"

"I love them! I wish I had some like that." Already, she was imagining what it would be like to have a sweet, smart daughter like Libby, one who had Wymon's eyes and his heartbreaking smile that melted her bones. But a boy would be wonderful, too. Two of each, maybe. Hopefully.

Wymon came back with some food and her drink. He sat down on the other side of her and put his arm around her shoulders. She took a few sips to convince him she was all right, but she was craving bed. This last month she'd been especially tired, and sleep seemed to be the panacea for her nausea.

While everyone ate, Eli got hold of Toly and handed the phone to Wymon. "It's on speaker, so everyone can hear." He'd forced Wymon to let go of Jasmine so he could stand up.

"Toly? How are you?" Wymon said.

"Great! Sounds like a fun Halloween party is going on. Wish I was there."

"We wish the same thing." He eyed Jasmine. "My wife and I have news. We're pregnant!"

"Whoopee!" Toly whistled, and it resounded throughout the living room. "Way to go, Jasmine Clayton! Another little rodeo champion is on the way. That makes three so far. I think we need to make it an even four. Roce? It's your turn next. You'd better get busy!"

"Not me, bro."

"That's what Wymon said until he ended up at the hospital hanging out with the hottie he rescued from the plane crash," Toly said. "When I talked to Solana, she told me Wymon was such a goner, he didn't know what day it was. Luis said he was worthless. Hey, big bro—if you're still listening, we all know how hard you fell. So did Mills. He hasn't recovered yet and wants to know if your wife has a sister."

Another laugh escaped Jasmine's lips.

"My wife is one of a kind," Wymon said with a tremor in his voice she felt deep inside.

"This is the best news I could possibly get this close to the rodeo finals. I couldn't be happier. Are you going to name him after me?"

For the first time all night Wymon broke into a smile. "What if it's a girl?"

"Well, how about Tolina?"

Everyone broke into laughter, including Jasmine. He'd just reminded her of her conversation with Wymon after she'd bought Moondrop. Wymon had suggested she name her new horse Percette instead of Perce. Like their good looks, a clever streak appeared to run in the Clayton family.

"I think Jasmine and I will have to think about

that one, Toly. Keep us posted about your next rodeo. We'll talk soon."

"I promise."

After Wymon got off the phone he turned to Jasmine. "It's time to take you home. Our neighbors will be showing up any minute. I'd rather leave before it becomes pure chaos around here."

That sounded good to Jasmine. She thanked everyone before Wymon helped her out of the house to the car. Sure enough, she saw four cars driving up the mountain road at that very moment. As much as she would have loved to see their friends, this wasn't the time.

Once they arrived back at their house, Wymon carried her inside and put her to bed where she took another pill. After his shower, he slid in next to her. She felt his hand rove over her body.

"I realize I can't feel our baby yet, but I know it's there."

She kissed his cheek. "It's a miracle, isn't it?"

"Yes." His voice shook. "Are you too nauseated for me to wrap you in my arms?"

"No," she answered honestly. "The medicine is beginning to work and I've never been happier in my life. Hold me and love me all night long. I need you so terribly. Do you know while we were talking in the hospital cafeteria that first day, I saw this magnificent man seated across from me and knew I wanted you for my husband."

*"Jasmine..."* He kissed her. "The same thing happened to me when I carried you away from the plane.

This heavenly creature I held in my arms was so beautiful and so courageous, I didn't know anyone like you existed. I wanted you in my life, in my heart. Roce said it was meant to be."

"He was so right." She buried her face in his neck and clung to him.

\* \* \* \* \*

*Watch for the next book in Rebecca Winters's* SAPPHIRE MOUNTAIN COWBOYS *miniseries,* COWBOY DOCTOR, *coming August 2017 only from Harlequin Western Romance!*

SPECIAL EXCERPT FROM

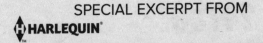

**HARLEQUIN®**

# Western Romance

*Sage Lockhart and Nick Monroe are friends with
benefits. When Sage asks Nick to make her dream of
having a family come true, he agrees…only because he
is secretly in love with her!*

*Read on for a sneak preview of*
*WANTED: TEXAS DADDY,*
*the latest book in Cathy Gillen Thacker's series*
***TEXAS LEGACIES: THE LOCKHARTS.***

"You want to have my baby," Nick Monroe repeated slowly, leading the two saddled horses out of the stables.

Sage Lockhart slid a booted foot into the stirrup and swung herself up. She'd figured the Monroe Ranch was the perfect place to have this discussion. Not only was it Nick's ancestral home, but with Nick the only one living there now, it was completely private.

She drew her flat-brimmed hat straight across her brow. "An unexpected request, I know."

Yet, she realized as she studied him, noting that the color of his eyes was the same deep blue as the big Texas sky above, he didn't look all that shocked.

For he better than anyone knew how much she wanted a child. They'd grown quite close ever since she'd returned to Texas, to claim her inheritance from her late father and help her mother weather a scandal that had rocked the Lockhart family to the core.

She drew a deep, bolstering breath. "The idea of a complete stranger fathering my child is becoming increasingly unappealing." When they reached their favorite picnic spot, she swung herself out of the saddle and watched as Nick tied their horses to a tree.

Nick grinned, as if pleased to hear she was a one-man woman, at least in this respect.

He looked at her from beneath the brim of his hat. "Which is why you're asking me?" he countered in the rough, sexy tone she'd fallen in love with the first second she had heard it. "Because you know me?"

Sage locked eyes with him, not sure whether he was teasing her or not. One thing she knew for sure: there hadn't been a time since they'd first met that she *hadn't* wanted him.

"Or because," he continued flirtatiously, as he unscrewed the lid on his thermos, "you have a hankering for my DNA?"

Aware the only appetite she had now was not for food, she quipped, "How about both?"

*Don't miss WANTED: TEXAS DADDY*
*by Cathy Gillen Thacker, available June 2017 wherever*
*Harlequin® Western Romance*
*books and ebooks are sold.*

www.Harlequin.com

HWREXP0517

Turn your love of reading into
rewards you'll love with

# Harlequin My Rewards

**Join for FREE today at
www.HarlequinMyRewards.com**

Earn **FREE BOOKS** of your choice.

Experience **EXCLUSIVE OFFERS** and contests.

Enjoy **BOOK RECOMMENDATIONS**
selected just for you.

**PLUS!** Sign up now
and get **500** points
right away!

Earn
**FREE**
REWARDS
HarlequinMyRewards.com
Join
Today!

MYR16R